"Cooperate t
Jordan warn

He pulled her close as they started to dance, adding, "Or we'll pack this charade in."

Cassy felt Jordan's lips on her cheek, moving closer to her mouth, and then his mouth closed over hers. She'd been willing to cooperate, but she'd never expected to cooperate so well.

His mouth suddenly hardened to possessiveness, the kiss deepening, and shock waves of feeling hit her deep inside, making her lips part involuntarily. Jordan took advantage of her weakness and stopped pretending to dance at all, and concentrated on the kiss.

Cassy became aware that the music had stopped and that they were the center of attention. Color flooded her face as Jordan turned her toward their table.

"Well," he murmured, "if that doesn't convince them you're taken, nothing will!"

PATRICIA WILSON used to live in Yorkshire, England, but with her children all grown up, she decided to give up her teaching position there and accompany her husband on an extended trip to Spain. Their travels are providing her with plenty of inspiration for her romance writing.

Books by Patricia Wilson

HARLEQUIN PRESENTS

934—THE FINAL PRICE
1062—A LINGERING MELODY
1086—THE ORTIGA MARRIAGE
1110—A MOMENT OF ANGER
1125—IMPOSSIBLE BARGAIN
1150—BELOVED INTRUDER
1174—A CERTAIN AFFECTION
1198—WHEN THE GODS CHOOSE
1221—THE GATHERING DARKNESS
1238—TEMPORARY BRIDE
1262—GUARDIAN ANGEL
1286—DANGEROUS OBSESSION

HARLEQUIN ROMANCE

2856—BRIDE OF DIAZ

PATRICIA WILSON

a secret understanding

Harlequin Books

TORONTO • NEW YORK • LONDON
AMSTERDAM • PARIS • SYDNEY • HAMBURG
STOCKHOLM • ATHENS • TOKYO • MILAN

Harlequin Presents first edition October 1990
ISBN 0-373-11310-2

Original hardcover edition published in 1989
by Mills & Boon Limited

Printed in U.S.A.

CHAPTER ONE

'IT'S time for the morning conference, Cassy.'

Guy Meredith looked across at Cassy and smiled ruefully. He knew as well as she did that it was unavoidable, but he also knew that she hated stepping into the editor's office now.

'I'll go instead if you can come up with an excuse,' he ventured, but she shook her head and began to gather her notes and pictures methodically. She might have to go, but she didn't have to rush.

'No, Guy. It's my job as features editor, the master expects it, I'll go. Chase up that picture of the common, the one that Patrick did in the spring. We'll start putting that feature together when I get back.'

The other heads of department were already across at the editor's office, but Cassy refused to hurry. She had the decided impression that Jordan Reece clocked her in each morning, and to face him at all was an irritation of the first order. It was still unbelievable that one man had managed to make such a change. At first it had seemed that every journalist on the *Bradbury Herald* had been ranged opposite him ready to fight any new innovation, but now they seemed very well pleased; only Cassandra Preston was out on a limb, and she had done nothing at all!

She had been part of the world of the Press for a good while now, starting with the Reece Group of newspapers as a very green reporter straight from university. Harold Reece was a wonderful man. He had helped her enormously, encouraging her in everything, giving her confidence. At twenty-five she had become features editor and she was good at her job, popular in the town, with plenty of contacts she had built up over her stay, and she was full of ideas. When Harold Reece retired, Cassy's nerve had almost deserted her as she saw his replacement.

Jordan Reece was not like his father in any way, and everyone knew as soon as they saw him that he would not be simply content to follow on, to continue a dynasty. He was already famous himself and he wouldn't be here long, everyone knew that. Life must be very dull for him in Bradbury after working as an overseas correspondent for television. Before long the Reece Group would put in a new editor and Jordan Reece would be back overseas reporting on some troubled area of the world. For now, though, he was still here and had to be faced daily.

She walked across to his office, but she was just a little late and he caught her again.

'Miss Preston!'

How did he manage to make her legs shake just by saying her name? He wasn't even angry! He was never angry. It was something in his tone, some deep, dark quality that contained censure even when he merely wanted her to do something. He was standing in the door of his own private office, looking too big for the building and too big for the job he was temporarily doing.

'When you're ready, please,' he ordered, with no smile at all.

He had always looked so handsome and powerful on television, quite the heart-throb when Cassy was at college. Some of the girls had even rushed out and bought his latest book, more for the photograph of him on the back than for the exciting and often painful accounts inside.

Cassy had read his books, though, and she had wondered if he was unhappy himself. Maybe it wasn't just that he took pleasure in remonstrating with her on every possible occasion? The others in the office escaped that more often than not. He called them by their names, their first names. She was 'Miss Preston!'. She could hear the hard voice in her sleep, see the silver eyes like two pools of ice. He had spoiled everything for her.

He waited at the door, standing there no doubt to quell any high spirits before she got into the conference. She knew that he disliked her for some reason, and it was probably her looks. Her brown eyes were sparky and determined, edged with thick black lashes. Her mouth curved into laughter easily, and her pert, heart-shaped face most certainly did have a rebellious look about it. Maybe that was what Jordan Reece disliked? Maybe he expected insubordination? He didn't approve of her clothes, either. His eyes skimmed over her short skirt and the long length of her legs with a barely concealed reprimand, and she looked back defiantly before he stepped aside and motioned her into his office.

It had been his father's office, and she always looked around with resentment when she was in here now. It was not the pleasant, rather scruffy place it had been, either; Jordan Reece had altered all that. It was now like stepping into a hospital ward, or the dentist's. Everything gleamed! The books on the shelves were strictly functional: trade journals, gazettes. The plants were green and alive, not the old dusty things that his father always forgot to water.

The fishing pictures had gone, too. She resented that most of all. Harold Reece was a keen fisherman, fanatical. He had often sat back in his chair and drifted into the world of glittering water and lurking trout, quite forgetting the matter at hand, but everything had managed to get itself done all the same and everyone had been happy. They were happy now in an uneasy sort of way, but she wasn't! She tossed back her hair, unruly curls the colour of mahogany, long and gleaming. If the worst came to the worst, there were other papers to work on.

'Perhaps we can begin now?'

Jordan Reece looked at his watch and then glanced pointedly at Cassy, but she stared straight back. One of these days she was simply going to walk out on him in mid-sentence!

She raised her eyebrows questioningly, but he frowned at her and walked round to his chair, sitting and tilting it back at an alarming angle. He continued to stare at her for a few disconcerting moments, making everyone else uncomfortable, and she tried to think of something to take her mind off him, something to make her keep this bouncing spirit. He made every day a battle.

'Would you like to begin, Miss Preston?' he asked coldly. 'What's happening about that hospital business?'

'It continues,' Cassy said crisply. 'That hospital business' was a very big campaign, a battle for rights. 'The local Health Authority wrote yesterday complaining about last week's feature, but it continues this week. They admit the chaos in the gynaecological department, but they suggest that it's none of our business!'

'Let me see the letter.'

Cassy handed it across to him; she had been expecting that. If he said it was to be dropped, she would resign. His eyes skimmed it and she held her breath.

'You can answer that yourself,' he murmured. 'You've got a waspish pen. See how they like that!'

Cassy felt a mixture of relief and rage. A waspish pen? He made her sound like an old spinster writing poison-pen letters!

'What's new?' he asked briefly, his eyes on her mutinous face. She wished that chair would slip. He must be almost on the point of balance. Just one more inch!

'I heard a whisper of news a few days ago and I've just confirmed it this morning at the Council offices. You probably know that our small neighbour, Risewell, comes under the Bradbury council for most things?'

He nodded, looking seriously at her, but saying nothing.

'Well, they pay their rates here although they get less service, and now it seems Bradbury is stealing from its small neighbour!'

'I'm intrigued.' The chair came back to its four legs and Jordan Reece leaned forward, his arms folded on his desk. He had his sleeves rolled up, his tie pulled away at the neck, the top button of his shirt unfastened, and for a second she stared at him, forgetting what she was going to say.

'Go on,' he urged softly.

'Well,' Cassy said quickly, pulling herself together, 'I thought in the spring that the common was a little extra resplendent, more crocuses than usual,' she added, referring to the great sweep of well-kept green belt that almost surrounded the town. 'Apparently, our Parks Department snaffled them from Risewell.'

Claud Ackland, the news editor, gave one of his irritating titters and chimed in. 'I've no complaints! I live facing the common. It was a picture in the spring.'

'We've got the picture!' Cassy bit out. 'And one of the previous spring. The second shows an unprecedented growth in crocuses, proof positive!'

'You're sure of this?' The editor's stern mouth quirked, suspiciously close to laughter, and Cassy felt furious. It must be very small and petty to someone who normally reported battles, who ducked bullets as he faced the cameras, but it was important to the people of Risewell, who had been outraged.

'I'm quite sure. My source is from the Council Chamber itself.'

He nodded, his eyes intently on her face. 'So what are you going to do with this item?'

'It will make the basis for a good feature. Our circulation is good in Risewell too, and in any case, just because we're the big neighbour, we have no right to take what few amenities they have. It's not the first time that something like this has happened. I've got plenty of information—verified!' she added smartly when his dark eyebrows rose.

He nodded, his silvery eyes narrowed at her aggressive look. 'Go to it!' he said evenly. She was going to, anyway!

The rest of the conference got under way and she was glad to be able to sit back and only add her bit when necessary. She found herself doing what she did every morning when she was in here: watching him. It was becoming something of a secret pastime.

His hands were powerful, capable, with a sort of hard, masculine grace. He wasn't as tanned now as he had been at first, but he was still a deep golden colour and it showed up those strange eyes vividly.

He looked up and caught her gaze, and she hastily gathered her things as the rest of the heads of department stood.

'Wait behind for a moment, Miss Preston,' Jordan Reece said quietly, and she sat down again worriedly. He was going to battle with her! She geared herself up, and she was quite right.

As soon as the others had left he held up last night's copy of the paper, opened at her theatre review.

'This is vicious, caustic, biased!' he said coldly. 'I would have thought that with your background you would have had sympathy for theatre people in general, and actors in particular!'

It was the last thing she wanted to hear. 'Actor' was a word that brought back too many memories, too much pain. Her face went quite pale and she blazed at him furiously, quite forgetting to be intimidated.

'I'm never *biased*!' she flared. 'The theatre here is good because they're constantly held to account.'

'You expect West End standards in Bradbury?' he insisted relentlessly.

'I expect value for money anywhere,' Cassy snapped. 'When they do well, they get a good write-up. If they produce a fiasco, then they should expect to be reported equally truthfully. I've never known them fail to send me tickets! It's not the first time that I've slated them! Your father never complained!' she ended bitterly. 'He left me to get on with things without constant comment and interference.'

He merely waved his hand towards the door, dismissing her. 'That's because you're not a trout. Things without gills are invisible to my father. In any case, I know you were his whiz-kid. He would never have questioned you.'

'If you're suggesting that your father let me just do anything and...'

'Why do you keep the theatre reviews for yourself?' he interrupted with a quick look at her from beneath dark brows, his silver eyes intent. 'You've plenty to do. Any feature writer could do it!'

'I prefer to do it myself!' Cassy said tightly.

He just looked at her for a long moment and then nodded, dismissing the conversation.

'Shall you use the new colour supplement for your feature about the Parks Department?' he asked ironically, as if it was a garden feature instead of a piece of serious investigative reporting.

'No! Before I've finished with it, the features department will have taken over the whole front page!'

'Really?' he said slowly, as if he was humouring a child. 'I suppose you've even got the headline?'

'Pillaging a village!' she snapped off the top of her head, walking out whether he'd finished with her or not, only just stopping herself from slamming the door.

'What did he want?' Claud Ackland looked at her red face with a great deal of interest as she passed him.

'I'd rather not say.'

'Oooh! Naughty man!' His low whistle infuriated her further, but she ignored him, walking quickly to the end of the office and her own little niche, sitting at her terminal for a minute to get her temper back before she tackled Guy about the new feature.

When she next went to the theatre, though, it was her second visit in one week. They always sent her two complimentary tickets so that she could bring a friend, but she never bothered. It was work as far as Cassy was concerned, and this time she was doing it twice. She had read last week's review and it *was* caustic! This week she wanted to be quite sure that her past was not raising its head and making her unfair. Her review was already written, in her bag at this moment, and she could see nothing wrong with it as the first half of the performance drew to a close. It was as bad as she had thought it the first time round!

In the bar she ordered a drink, accustomed to being alone and feeling no embarrassment. The deep voice that added to her order and the powerful, brown hand that slid the money across the counter to pay for both made her jump, her nerves flaring frighteningly.

'I was in the dress circle,' Jordan Reece said warningly as he led her to a table. 'I was watching you all the time, and as far as I could see you never made one single note. You have total recall, Miss Preston?'

'I don't need it tonight!' she snapped, her sparky brown eyes furious at this spying. 'This is the second time around. I was here two nights ago. My review is written and in my bag at this moment.'

'Then you don't count yourself infallible? May I see it?'

She hadn't much choice, his hand was out ready, total obedience expected, and she dived into her bag and slapped her shorthand notebook into his imperious hand, quite sure that by now, he would have forgotten any shorthand he had ever known, for his life was so far removed from such mundane matters.

He hadn't. He read it swiftly, his eyes flying over the neat marks on each page, his brief comments showing that he understood perfectly well everything he read.

'I can see that you're no more impressed with this week's performance than you were with the one last week,' he observed as he handed the notebook back.

'Were you?' Cassy asked tartly.

'Candidly, I thought it was dreadful,' he admitted. 'If I hadn't been watching you, I would probably have fallen asleep!'

That did not please her much. The idea of being followed and checked like a raw junior made her blood boil. The bell for the end of the interlude sounded and she gathered her bag.

'Shall we give it a miss?' he asked hopefully, and for one moment she considered saying 'Certainly not!' making him go back to face utter boredom now he realised that spying on her was a waste of time. She didn't fancy sitting through any more, though, so she shrugged indifferently and led the way to the street.

He paced along beside her and she couldn't think how to get rid of him politely. It had been raining while they had been in the theatre, and the streets were wet and shining, the lights shimmering on the wet pavements. The embarrassment of walking beside him was eased a little as passers-by recognised her and called out to her, but even so she had to curb the inclination to take to her heels. It was bad enough to have to face him at work. This was an extraneous activity she could well have managed without!

'How long have you been here?' he asked when the next person called out cheerfully to her. 'You seem to know everyone.'

'I came here straight from university,' she said briefly. 'I like it here.'

'It's a long way from home, isn't it?' he pried quietly. 'I'm rather surprised that you decided to be a journalist when your family are theatre through and through.'

'I didn't want to tread the same path!' she said sharply, the mention of her family making her feel icily cold. It was a topic she never raised, not even to herself.

'I see that your mother is appearing in the West End,' he went on, not knowing that he was twisting a knife deeper and deeper into her. She had to remind herself that he didn't know, that nobody knew. He was not getting at her again; it was just unfortunate. 'I've not heard of your father for a long time. Was he in New York with your mother when she was there?'

'They never travel together,' Cassy said tightly. 'They never have done. Acting always separated them. They're used to it. My father is—resting!' she ended, with a scathing sound to her voice that brought his silvery eyes sharply to her face.

‘You did a lot of drama at university,’ hc said quictly, no doubt thinking that he was changing the conversation at the sharp sound of her voice. He was merely grinding things in deeper.

‘You’re very well informed, Mr Reece,’ Cassy observed, and it seemed to bring him to the realisation that he could talk all night and get nothing but stiff replies.

‘You have a file, Miss Preston,’ he said quite coldly, ‘and apart from that, you were my father’s “blue-eyed girl”. When I visit him, I’m expected to report on your progress!’

‘‘That’s why you harass me?’ Cassy asked scornfully, the hurt she was feeling inside too much to contain, although it had nothing to do with Jordan Reece.

‘No, I just like to see that you toe the line!’ he said irritably. ‘You get no more attention than anyone else. I have a job to do, too.’

‘Even though you resent it!’ she finished for him, unable to stop herself.

‘Even though I resent it,’ he agreed. ‘I won’t escort you any further,’ he added irascibly. ‘By the number of people you know, I very much doubt if you’re going to be attacked. We’re almost at your flat, and in any case you have a very sharp weapon in your tongue. All they would get from you would be a headline!’

He turned on his heel and walked back the way they had come. He had obviously parked his car by the theatre and walked this far to escort her. Cassy felt waves of guilt sweeping over her. She turned to say that she was sorry, but he was already well down the road, tall, dark and back to being unapproachable. She went to her flat severely chastened, her own misery forgotten in a flurry of embarrassment at her bad temper and even worse manners.

The morning's post brought a letter, and at first Cassy paid no particular attention to it. She had strict rules about mail, she read it as she ate breakfast, so the letter lay on the table as she got ready and prepared her toast and coffee. She had not the slightest premonition as she picked it up, her cup in her other hand, her eyes scanning the envelope almost casually. It was her home postmark, but the address was typed; it couldn't be from her father and it certainly would not be from her mother! She pushed the thought of her mother firmly away. She had troubles enough as it was. It had to be a bill. She opened it with no enthusiasm whatever and glanced at it, then stopped, her face going pale.

After reading it through twice, she still felt quite numb with shock, and only the thought of being late and the opportunity it would give Jordan Reece to reprimand her made her get to her feet and reach for her coat and bag. Inside her head she was frantic. She had no idea what she was going to do. So much for premonition!

The letter *was* from her mother, or at least from her mother's secretary, for Lavinia Preston did not bother to write personal letters any more. She would be at home this weekend, a brief stop-over before going on to New York for the opening of her new play on Broadway. She expected that Cassy would be able to get down to see them, and Cassy knew that 'them' did not mean her mother and father, it meant her mother and Luigi.

She walked to work in deep thought, even walking past the building and having to re-trace her steps.

'Forgotten where you work, Miss Preston?'

Jordan Reece's sardonic voice made her jump, and for once her eyes were not smiling, either impudently or otherwise. They were not angry, either. They were dazed and scared. He was just getting out of his car, a Porsche Carrera, bright red and alarmingly sleek. He was certainly too big for his job, too big for this town and too expensive. For a moment her mind switched from her personal nightmare and she found herself really looking at him.

She remembered the first time he had come into the office. Harold Reece had brought him round, politely introducing him to the staff, and he had not bent one inch. Her first sight of him had shocked her. She had never seen a man so handsome and so hard.

He had been very tanned then, obviously straight back from some overseas assignment. His dark hair was thick and heavy, his cheeks creased as though he laughed a lot, although she had never seen it happen, but those cold, silver eyes had alarmed her. He looked at everyone steadily as if taking some uninteresting inventory, his nod brief and polite, his handshake firm. His hand had almost swallowed her own smaller hand and she had been very pleased when he'd moved on. She had known straight away that she could never get on with him. In everything, he was the exact opposite to her. She had been so perfectly right!

'If you could reach some kind of decision about going into the building...?' He was standing holding the door for her and she felt perfectly foolish. She had been standing staring at him, her mind elsewhere, and it wasn't like her at all. It was the letter, her panic!

'Sorry. I was thinking about—about something else...' She darted inside with a quick little nod of thanks and he said nothing at all. She could feel his eyes on her as she went up the stairs in front of him, and she was glad when she reached the top and the main door. Guy Meredith opened his mouth to say something, but closed it again as he saw the editor come in at the same time, opening the door for her. He shook himself out of the surprise, though.

'Got your theatre review, Cassy?' he asked, and when she nodded he gestured to her desk. 'Two tickets have come for you, next week's. Who do you take, the boyfriend?'

'Naturally!' Cassy sank down at her desk, fumbling in her bag as Jordan Reece walked past to his office. Boyfriend! The words 'theatre' and 'boyfriend' could still bring back hurt, shame, although it should have been quite gone by now. It was a long time, after all. It was the last thing she wanted to think of. Still, she didn't have to go home. She could simply not answer, or plead pressure of work. Even as she thought it, she knew perfectly well that she could not. She had never ducked out of anything in her life, and she could just see the amused contempt on her mother's face.

It was at university that Cassy had met Luigi Rosato. He had only just come from Italy then. He was thirty, much older than the other students, and he had fascinated them, especially the girls. His dark good looks and his very Latin manners had made him the most eligible man on the campus, and he was so *nice*! He never tired of listening to everyone's problems. It was a source of amusement to him that Cassy never had any problems at all, that she was merely good company.

He had been part of the theatre workshop group where Cassy spent most of her spare time, and he was an excellent actor. With a mother and father who were both in the theatre, Cassy recognised his talent and encouraged him all the time.

It drew them together, finally very closely together, and Luigi's days as an eligible bachelor were counted as over by the other students. As for Cassy, she was completely happy and completely in love. It seemed that nothing could burst her bubble of happiness when she took Luigi home for the long summer vacation. It was the end of her dreams. Her mother had been there, a flying visit between rehearsals, but after taking one look at Luigi Lavinia Preston had stayed on.

There was not much feeling between her parents, Cassy had known that since her very young days. Her father had not had Lavinia's success. He was a character actor, and although he worked regularly he knew himself that he did not and would never have the stunning brilliance of his wife. Cassy was not close to either of them. She had always been just a little in the way, her life ruled by a succession of nannies until she was old enough for boarding-school. She felt closer to Luigi than she had ever felt to her parents.

It had taken a while to realise what was happening, to understand that her beautiful, talented mother was deliberately staying behind in the country, ignoring the glitter of her own life-style to stay on here—for Luigi! It had seemed ridiculous. He was younger by twelve years, but her mother had never hidden the fact that she had lovers and she was beautiful, her hair fiery where Cassy's was deeply rich, her eyes brilliantly green against Cassy's sparky brown—and she had years of experience, great acting ability.

When they returned to university, Luigi left almost at once, dropping a course that had never particularly interested him, and when the newspapers came out a week later, Lavinia Preston was on the front page—British stage star boarding her flight to New York, Luigi smiling and handsome beside her. It was not every girl who could say that her mother had stolen her sweetheart—stolen him deliberately and skilfully. It had almost broken Cassy's heart, and now Lavinia was back, Luigi with her, expecting a nice home reunion!

It had been four years ago, but it seemed like yesterday. He had not made the impact on New York that he had so clearly imagined, but then, he didn't need to. Lavinia was clever in more ways than one. She was rich, nothing squandered, her investments solid and safe. Luigi could live like a prince and do nothing at all except be a handsome, attentive escort. Her mother would dangle the carrot of large parts in plays in front of him forever, as she had done when she had first met him, and he would believe every word.

The love that Cassy had felt was now deeply edged with contempt, but she did not have the courage to face them, not even after so long. She would never have the courage to face her mother's knowingly amused eyes, her father's utter indifference and Luigi's insincere protests of fate.

'Miss Preston!'

Oh, lord, she had been working and dreaming at the same time! Cassy shot up in her seat, her eyes anxiously on her terminal, astonished to see that she had finished the feature and that it had gone off screen. What had she done? No doubt she was about to find out. She walked to Jordan Reece's office on trembling legs.

'What's the matter with you?' he exclaimed angrily. 'I may take you to task for caustic comment, for bias and even for the sharpness of your tongue, but you never make mistakes!'

'What—what have I done?' Cassy just stood looking at him in a panic-stricken way, and he grunted irritably, waving her to a chair.

'Sit down before you fall down,' he rasped. 'I've been looking at your feature, as it so intrigued me. It was full of ridiculous errors, so much so that I expected to see you slumped in your chair semi-conscious!'

'Oh, it's gone through to typeset! I'll miss my deadline!'

Cassy shot to her feet, but he motioned her back impatiently, pointing to his own terminal.

'I corrected it and then sent it through,' he snapped. 'The whole thing was excellent, but peppered with weird mistakes! Eric Brown would have been the laughing stock of the Council if he had been printed as Miss Brown! What's the matter with you? I've made a list of your errors, take a look.'

He held up a sheet of paper, a long list of mistakes on it that almost reached the bottom of the sheet, and Cassy's face flooded with colour, her ego utterly flattened. She didn't have any explanation that she was prepared to give, and after a long, disgruntled look at her he allowed her to make her escape.

She lingered at her desk when the paper was safely 'put to bed'. The others had gone and the only light was over her own desk. In the quiet building she still failed to find any solution to her problem; there was no solution. If she refused to go, then her mother would know she had won, how much it had hurt. Luigi would be tenderly and insincerely sorry, her father wouldn't give a damn! If she went, could she face them? Could she convince them of her own success, her utter nonchalance about the past? There was no nonchalance there, and she was not at all happy about her own acting ability.

'There's something wrong, isn't there?' The deep voice, no longer harsh, made her jump, and she realised belatedly that Jordan Reece was invariably the last person to leave the Herald building.

'I—er—no!' She was filled with embarrassment and confusion, but he didn't take much notice. He reached forward and switched off her light, picking up her bag and handing it to her.

'Get your coat, Cassandra,' he ordered firmly, 'You and I are going to that tea shop on the corner for a nice, hot cup of tea.'

'But I—I don't . . .' She was stunned to have acquired a Christian name and, protests ignored, he took her arm, almost marching her to the street.

'I do!' he said firmly. 'Besides, I have something to tell you, and now is as good a time as any.'

He was going to ask for her resignation, she just knew it. He thought that she would need a soothing beverage to take the blow. She would need more than a cup of tea after this dreadful day!

'I see they've got the Christmas lights up on the edge of the common already,' he said in a pleasant voice, looking out towards the end of town. 'Let's hope they didn't snaffle any of those from Risewell, or they'll be taking them down rapidly and giving them back when your feature hits the news-stands. It even filled me with righteous indignation, and I've never even driven as far as Risewell!'

He was talking to calm her, to keep her captured, she could tell that. Not that he needed to. His hand was tightly on her arm and, although she was tall herself, he made her feel pretty insignificant as he walked her along, towering over her. Whatever he was going to say, he had no intention of her escaping. She was going to hear it whether she wanted to or not!

CHAPTER TWO

CASSY wished the tea shop had been crowded, making any confidential conversation impossible, but it was not. There were only three people in the whole place, counting the waitress, and Jordan led her to the farthest corner, well away from even these prying eyes. When the tea was ordered he sat back and looked at her severely, and she knew straight away that she had a battle on her hands, that this man was even more of a determined character than she was herself.

'Since I came to the *Herald*,' he said quietly, 'you have resented me, presumably because I'm not my father. You have skirted on the very edge of defying every last order I've given. You've made a very conscious decision not to co-operate unless it was absolutely necessary. Every morning conference is a battleground to you as you wait to cross swords with me.'

There was not a lot that Cassy could say to that, lying not being one of her accomplishments, and after a disgruntled look at her he continued.

'During today it has become increasingly clear that something is very wrong, apart from your general dislike of me. Now, I'm not going to attempt to be either fatherly or friendly, but even with your ability to go stubbornly on your own way, you must see that it's my duty to be concerned, especially when I find myself correcting your mistakes.'

'It won't happen again,' Cassy said quickly, meeting his cool-eyed stare and then as quickly ducking her head. 'I had some news that upset me, that's all. I obviously won't go on being upset. It's Thursday today. I only have to get through tomorrow and then I'll have the whole weekend to solve my problem.'

'So, we have established that you have a problem, that you refuse help and that by Monday morning you're going to be right back to normal—irritating!' he rasped.

'Yes. If you think that's normal!' Cassy shot back with an annoyed look at him.

'Oh, I don't think it's *normal*, Miss Preston,' he assured her. 'It's the situation we find ourselves in.'

She was back to being Miss Preston, she noted, and she smiled wanly at the waitress and proceeded to pour the tea, silence seeming to be a good idea.

'Well, as we seem to have reached the end of that voyage of discovery,' he remarked after a few moments of silence, during which he stared at her impatiently, 'I'll tell you why I wanted a quiet word with you.'

Here it comes, Cassy thought, bracing herself for attack, but his words and changed tone surprised her into looking up with wide, shocked eyes.

'My father has to go into hospital next weekend. He needs an operation that's long overdue,' Jordan told her quietly.

'Oh, I'm sorry! I had no idea!' Cassy was filled with sympathy and anxiety at once. Harold Reece had meant a lot to her. In many ways he had become the father she would have liked, someone who helped, who listened kindly and amusedly to her problems and suggested solutions. It was Harold Reece who had steadied her, knowing she had a secret grief, never asking about it but simply being on hand with his ready smile when she felt low.

'Believe me, he would never have handed over the reins if he had been well,' Jordan said with an amused smile.

'He sits at home with the fish portraits in his study and dreams of the *Herald*, I assure you.'

That bit of information made Cassy feel incredibly guilty. Of course he had taken his beloved pictures with him. She had decided bad-temperedly that Jordan Reece had thrown them out. She *was* biased!

'Is—is it very serious?' she asked softly, willing him to laugh and say no, but he didn't. He hesitated and then shrugged, his eyes cautious.

'We really don't know. A stomach operation is not pleasant for anyone, and he's no longer young.'

'Is there anything I can do?' Cassy said impulsively, and those silver-grey eyes were on her again, sharply focused and attentive.

'There is, if you really mean that. He wants to see you. This weekend is his last at home for a while, and he has this overwhelming desire to see his protégée. You know he was, still is, very fond of you. I brought you here to ask you to go down there with me this weekend, just to set his mind at rest before he goes into hospital. Will you come to convince him that you're still in one piece?'

The moment that she hesitated, his eyes cooled as contempt edged his firm mouth, and he gave her no time to speak.

'So you won't!' he grated. 'I might have known. Quite the hard-bitten journalist, aren't you?'

'You don't understand!' Cassy blurted desperately. 'I want to go. Your father was so important to me...'

'But not important enough to make an effort for now,' he interrupted sarcastically.

'Any weekend but this!' Cassy said urgently, ignoring his contempt. 'Next weekend I'll go gladly. I'll go to the hospital. I'll stay down there and visit every day.'

'That will be a little late for him to talk to you before he goes,' Jordan said coldly. 'This is to set his mind at rest. He has this urge to put his affairs in order and you're on the agenda. I'm sorry that it's not convenient!'

He put his cup down with the obvious intention of leaving, and Cassy looked at him with an acknowledgment of defeat.

'I'll come,' she said quietly, but it merely annoyed him more.

'Unwillingly? No, thank you!' he rasped. 'He can well do without people around him who couldn't care less!'

'You're quite cruel, aren't you?' Cassy asked shakily, her brown eyes fixed reproachfully on his hard face. 'I could never understand why I disliked you so much, but it's obvious really. You're cruel! You're not a bit like your father. You have no idea what he meant to me, and you have no idea why I hesitated to say yes straight off. You just attack!'

To her horror she felt tears flood into her eyes and she hastily looked away, sitting there in embarrassed silence, waiting for him to storm off.

'My father is a hard act to follow,' he said softly, 'and he had a lot of advantages over me, one being that you confided in him. There's not much point in my offering help to you, I've tried it and been told smartly to back off. Oh, not in so many words,' he added with a grimace as she looked up at him with tears sparkling in her eyes. 'I'm quick to take a hint, though, especially when it's hurled at me like a discus!'

'I—I'll go this weekend,' Cassy muttered, looking away. 'I want to go! I told you he means a lot to me and I meant it.'

'All right.' He signalled to the waitress and prepared to leave. 'We'll have to go in the middle of the afternoon, earlier if we can manage it. I'll get on the phone tonight and try to arrange for you to take tomorrow off. I'll collect you at about eleven if I can manage to get a replacement in for you.'

'But what will people...' Cassy began anxiously, blushing furiously at his quietly muttered opinion of people and their speculations. She was glad to be outside in the gathering dusk.

'I'll drive you to your flat, then I can be quite sure I have the right one tomorrow,' he said firmly as they walked across the road. 'I only know pretty vaguely where you live.'

'I'm pretty vague myself at the moment,' Cassy said thoughtlessly as he helped her into the opulent Porsche in front of the Herald Building and then got in himself, turning to her with an expression of near anger on his face.

'For heaven's sake Cassandra,' he bit out, 'I know how you care for my father. I know how you go in feet first with everything. Hesitating about something like that is just not you. Tell me what's wrong or I'll give some deep consideration to shaking you!'

He looked as if he meant it, and she was still feeling very guilty about that hesitation. It was important to her that he should realise how much she cared about his father.

'I had to go home this weekend,' she murmured, her eyes firmly on her hands, which were equally firmly in her lap. 'I—I don't often go but—but my mother wrote—at least, her secretary did. She's going to be there this weekend and—and I'd decided that I had to face her to let her know that...'

'I see,' he said quietly, and laughter bubbled up uncontrollably inside Cassy.

'Oh, no, you don't see,' she informed him a little wildly. 'You really don't! I mean, it's so unusual. It's not every mother who...'

She stopped, suddenly horrified at the fact that she had been about to blurt out her private affairs, and after one hard look at her Jordan started the engine and turned the car towards her flat. It took all the way to calm down, and even as he stopped outside she was still trembling.

'In view of the fact that you have some sort of crisis in your own life,' he said, obviously choosing his words with care, 'I apologise for my earlier remarks, and I'll tell my father that next weekend or the one after that I'll drive you down to see him.'

'No!' If the choice was Harold Reece and his peace of mind, or her mother's amused contempt, then she would choose Harold Reece every time. 'I'm going this weekend and they can think what they like about me at home!'

'You're sure?' he asked quietly, his eyes piercingly on her, noting her agitation.

'I'm quite sure,' Cassy said firmly, taking a deep breath and meeting his gaze.

'Then will you have dinner with me tonight? I think we should be a little better acquainted before my father begins snooping, don't you?'

The same old hesitation clouded her eyes and he looked not at all surprised.

'It was just an idea,' he said resignedly, starting the car.

If ever there was a man for making her feel guilty! She had misjudged him, been bordering on rude, blamed him for things he had not done at all and now she was treating him like this.

'I have a couple of steaks in the fridge,' she said quickly. 'I could make a salad without much effort and there's fruit. If you'd like to eat here with me, I...'

'I'm stunned,' he said, his smile growing by the minute. 'I'll be back in one hour with wine, will that do?'

'Yes, I—I'll get it started...'

'If you should come to your senses and change your mind,' he said softly, his smile mocking her, 'just leave a note on the door.'

He had driven off before she could reply, and Cassy went inside, a little dazed at her sudden burst of hospitality. It was the first time ever that she had invited a man to her flat, and even in her wildest imagination she had never thought of it being Jordan Reece. This was going to be some evening! She looked round worriedly and quickly got out the vacuum cleaner. What would just about do for her during the week would not do for him. She didn't want him going round with a duster.

By the time he returned she had cleaned and polished, had a shower and changed into an embroidered caftan she had been saving for a special occasion and the steaks were well on the way. As she was finishing the dressing for the salad, he came to the door and she was relieved to see that he had changed too, his dark suit gone and a casual outfit in its place. His eyes looked more silvery than ever against the black shirt, and they stood for a moment staring at each other.

'Mutual surprise!' he commented, coming straight through to the small kitchen with the wine. 'Can I set the table?'

'If you like.' Cassy pointed to the drawer that held the cutlery, and spread a blue checked cloth on the table before returning to the dressing. 'The—the glasses are up there in that cupboard. There aren't many, I don't have guests for dinner as a rule and I...'

'One each will be quite enough,' he said quietly. 'Don't be nervous, Cassandra. Honestly, I don't bite!'

'I'll be nervous if you keep on calling me Cassandra,' Cassy said, bending over the salad to hide her blushes. It would not have been so bad if he had been smaller. She already knew he was too big for the office. He filled the kitchen. This place was not meant to hold two tall people. He was making it seem like a doll's house.

'Cassandra,' he mused, opening the wine. 'A prophetess. What do you forecast for the steak?'

'Burned, if we don't eat at once!' Cassy said promptly, dishing it up and putting the salad on the table.

'It looks good enough to eat,' Jordan said with a certain amount of surprise, holding her chair for her.

'Anybody can cook a steak,' Cassy said firmly, determined not to let anything get friendly.

'If you believe that, you'll believe anything,' he said wryly, and Cassy decided to get through the meal and then talk seriously about his father. This was a one-off occasion and she didn't like being so close to this powerful man. He wasn't her type. She liked people who were softer, more gentle. She was normally suspicious of any sign of straightforward masculinity, and he couldn't help that, it was how he was. She was bending over backwards to be fair to him now, but the underlying thoughts were very edgy.

She watched him surreptitiously as she ate, looking at him from beneath thick lashes. She knew that she did that every day at the morning conferences, and she knew why. His aggressive masculinity repulsed her. She was always on her guard. Jordan Reece was too virile, almost tangibly so, and every defence came up whenever he was near. She heartily wished she had not invited him tonight, but as usual he had managed to put her at a disadvantage.

'Have you had this flat since you first came to thc town?' he asked with interest when they had finished and were drinking coffee in her small, neat sitting-room.

'No, I couldn't afford a flat then. It may have slipped your mind, but juniors don't earn much,' Cassy said, glancing at him. 'I shared a house with three other girls. We got on well enough, but I'd rather be alone, although I'm still quite friendly with all of them.'

'What do you do at the weekends?' he asked interestedly, his eyes keenly on her downcast face. He was sitting back in his chair, his legs stretched out comfortably as if he belonged here, and a brief flare of resentment clouded her eyes. Life had been good here before he came, and he certainly had brought bad luck. After four years she would have to face Luigi again. If Harold Reece had still been here she would have told him everything, and he would have come up with some obvious solution.

'This and that. I do my shopping and walk, and sometimes I go out with the girls I knew, the ones who shared the house with me,' she said shortly.

'No steady boyfriend?'

'No!' There was battle in Cassy's eyes at once and he smiled ruefully.

'Just general conversation, Cassy,' he said quietly. 'No prying intended. We'd better get on with the discussion about the weekend before I outstay my welcome. I arranged for a replacement. One of the subs will go in. I know it's not his job, but there's little enough to do; the work as far as you're concerned was finished today, and in any case, Guy will be there.'

'I'm sorry,' Cassy murmured. 'I suppose I'm a bit on edge. I never meant to make you feel unwelcome. I—would you like more coffee?'

'No, thanks,' he said briskly, his voice a little tight. 'Let's get down to this weekend.'

It was all a bit too much suddenly, the thought of her mother, Luigi, her father's bland indifference. Harold Reece was going into hospital and she really cared, but the weekend at home was still the thought at the top of her head and she was being really awful to Jordan Reece. She had been sitting here thinking bad thoughts about him and, after all, he had worse problems. If he hadn't cared about his father he would never have taken on the job as editor, she knew that deep down.

'Cassy?' It wasn't until Jordan spoke softly that she realised she was sitting with her head bent, tears rolling down her face. She couldn't look up at all. It was so utterly embarrassing, and she stiffened sharply when he came and sat beside her.

'Look,' he said quietly, 'if you want to cancel this thing and go home, then do it. Clearly this is something very important or you wouldn't be in this state.'

'No, I'm going to see your father! I don't care what they think. I'll just never go home again, that's all. It won't make much impression, whatever I do.'

He was silent for a moment and then said quietly, 'How about two birds with one stone? From your file it seems that you lived in Hampshire. We could visit your place on the way down. You could stay there Friday night and Saturday morning, and we could go on to Surrey on Saturday afternoon.'

'Oh, no!' Cassy looked up, hastily wiping away the tears. 'I could never have anyone else there when . . . I mean, it's something I have to do alone. I would be very embarrassed if you . . .'

He looked so weary at her vehemence, so resigned that she had flung the small kindness back in his face, that she let her pride go by and told him.

'My mother will be bringing someone with her,' she said looking away from his tight face. 'When I was at university, I—we—were going to be engaged. I took him home for the holidays and my mother was there.' She shrugged. 'That was it! They're going to be there this weekend, together. It's all very respectable on the surface, you realise?' she added with a bitter laugh. 'It's quite normal, after all, for an actress to have someone in tow, especially an actress as beautiful and talented as my mother, and even if Luigi is much younger than her, you'd never know it. She's quite lovely,' she finished quietly.

'I know, I've seen her,' Jordan said tautly. 'So why the reunion, Cassy? Is this to rub things in? To see how much you can take? She's got you in a fix, hasn't she? If you don't go, you're scared, still pining for Luigi. If you do go, every small sound, every look you give will be misconstrued. Are you still in love with him?'

'I don't know,' Cassy said quietly. It was true, she didn't. She felt contempt, disgust even, but if she saw him again, spoke to him, what then?

'Facing him is the only way you're going to find out,' Jordan said rather fiercely.

'I know that but...'

'But what if you love him still? What if it shows? There is a solution,' he said quietly. 'Take your own fiancé with you, give them one hell of a surprise!'

'I'd love to do that!' Cassy said bitterly. 'Unfortunately, you may not have noticed, but I just don't have one to hand.'

'I'll do the job most efficiently if you'll trust me with it,' he said in a matter-of-fact voice, 'and if you'll do something for me?'

'What?' She shot upright and stared and he smiled wryly.

'Is that a gasp or a question?' he asked sardonically. 'If it's a gasp, then don't jump to hasty conclusions! If it's a question, then make some more coffee and I'll tell you about my bargain and my plan.'

Actually, she couldn't wait to get into the kitchen and out of sight. He had insisted upon washing up earlier, before coffee, so there was no real excuse to linger. She made it last a long time, though, and when she summoned up enough nerve to go back in he was pacing about the room like a caged beast.

'You're not going to like this,' he said with a grim certainty. 'I know your ability to fly off the handle, but all I ask is that you hear me out first, all right?'

Cassy nodded and dealt with the coffee, and he didn't even sit down with his. He put it on the mantelpiece and stood there looking down at her, seeming to be very careful about choosing his words.

'You know what I did before I came here to take the paper over?' he asked suddenly.

'Yes, you were a foreign correspondent for television. We used to see you when I was at university.'

'That rather puts me in my place,' he said drily. 'You were a little girl when I was out there at first. I'm thirty-six.'

'I'm twenty-five, but I can't see what that's got to do with it,' Cassy commented. 'As to being a little girl, I was never that. I was taller than most people at college, including the men. Anyway, it looked very exciting and very dangerous at times.'

'Oh, it was,' he said quietly, a rather far-away look in his eyes. 'When you've lived on a high, fast plane, it takes a great effort to come down to earth. The *Bradbury Herald* has few high spots and no danger at all, except for the odd spat with you. You were quite right, I resented it, I still do at times.'

He suddenly sat down, his eyes intently on her face.

'My father built up this chain of papers. He was a reporter and worked his way up to managing editor of the *Bradbury Herald*. When it went up for sale, he bought it. He used everything he had, everything he could borrow, and it paid off. He built on from there. Nothing came easy for him, Cassy, and there were times when we were quite poor. University for me was rather a struggle, then I became a green reporter, badly paid, as you reminded me, then moved into radio and thence to television. He wanted me to come here and take over, but I liked what I was doing. I came very unwillingly when he retired, and only then because I knew he was ill. He doesn't want me to go back. He imagines that one day I'm not going to duck fast enough. He wants me to settle down, get married, stay here. It's another thing on his list of items for straightening his affairs before he goes into hospital.'

'Are you telling me that he thinks he'll never come out?' Cassy asked anxiously, her own problems now way to the back of her mind.

'He's in his late sixties. He's been putting this off for long enough. A stomach obstruction is not a pleasant thing, and I believe he thinks that they're not telling him the whole truth.'

'Are they?' Cassy asked worriedly.

'Yes, but he's uneasy in his mind. I'm a very devious character, Cassy,' Jordan confessed with a wry look at her. 'I took you to tea tonight to ask you to go down and see him, but later I was going to ask you to pretend to be engaged to me, just to set his mind at rest, to allow him to go into hospital with the idea that I'm settling down at last.'

It seemed a great deal more important than her reason for wanting an escort, but it was a shock all the same.

'Why me?' she asked in surprise. 'We don't even get on well together. Surely you've got a girlfriend or two who would meet the requirements more easily?'

'Nobody that he dotes on,' Jordan pointed out sardonically. 'I think he splits his affection between you and me. You probably have more than your share of it, too!'

'I don't know about this.'

Cassy jumped up and did a little pacing of her own, her arms folded tightly across her. To deceive her mother and Luigi was one thing, to deceive Harold Reece was something yet again.

'It can't be done!' she said decidedly. 'When he comes out of hospital he's going to be hurt beyond recall. He'll never trust either of us again. I can't do that to your father.'

'You can do it to your mother and this—Luigi,' he reminded her softly.

'That's different! As far as I'm concerned, it's self-defence with them—and in any case, I haven't agreed to it.'

'Yet,' he added for her quietly. 'In my father's case, he would go in happily knowing that I was staying to safeguard everything he's worked for. When he comes out it could be broken to him gently in a few months' time. We could say that we fight too much, which is quite true,' he added wryly.

'A few months?' Cassy stopped pacing and sat hurriedly. 'I never—I envisaged one day!'

'Oh, come on!' he said scathingly. 'Lavinia Preston is no fool, and she's a great actress. If she's to be convinced, then it's going to take more than you with an escort and a few small sighs! If she can't spot a poor performance, who can?'

It was true. Cassy had never looked at it like that, in fact she was still reeling from the idea. Even so, months! The thought of his father still troubled her too much also.

'I can't fool your father!' she said determinedly, but he had her looking uncertain at once.

'Not even to give him a little happiness and peace of mind to face an ordeal? Is it too much to ask of your conscience? It seems to me from what you've said that he means more to you than your own parents. Certainly, to him, you're the daughter he never had. I phoned your feature to him as it finished today, and he's bursting with pride. It's just the sort of thing he fought for himself when he was here. Your conscience or your affection, Cassy? It boils down to that.'

'I don't know if I can manage it,' Cassy said worriedly after a few moments of silence. 'I can spot bad acting, but that doesn't make me into an actress myself. My mother will know, probably your father will too.'

'I guarantee that your mother will not know,' he said grimly. 'All you have to do is blush and swoon; you can leave your mother and Luigi to me! I take it you *can* blush and swoon?' he added mockingly.

'Blush, yes, the swooning bit I can't be sure of,' Cassy said with a sudden smile.

All at once a burden seemed to be lifting, her fears receding. Jordan Reece was no mere boy to stand beside her and simper as she told a few lies. It was a comfort to know he would be there, and she was glad she had told him her worries.

'Your father, though...' she began, her smile dying.

'Leave that to time,' he said quietly. 'You have no reason to want a quick end to this engagement, have you?'

'Well—no, I don't suppose it matters, not really,' she said with a rueful look. She had steadfastly pushed away all interested males. After Luigi, she just did not trust any man except Harold Reece. She was placing plenty of trust in Jordan, though, but after all it was a mutual thing.

'Then tomorrow we'll go and face the music,' he said, standing ready to leave. 'Meanwhile, practise that rare and charming smile. You'll need it when you face your mother and—friend. Nobody knows about this, just you and I. She's not going to find out, believe me!'

Cassy nodded, still a little worried, but he smiled down at her at the door and already it seemed that they had an understanding, a secret one. She was glad not to be going in to the office tomorrow. She wasn't really cut out for subterfuge.

CHAPTER THREE

CASSY was nervous the next day as she saw the Porsche stop in front of the flat. She stood by the window and watched Jordan Reece get out. He looked a little grim, and she knew without doubt that he was liking this no more than she was. She had wondered if he would arrive in casual clothes, her nervousness making her uncertain as to what to wear. He was not in any way casual, however; his dark grey suit was beautifully tailored, his shirt crisply white, and she had to admit that he was a very handsome, striking man; but he was very remote-looking, nothing friendly about him, and she wondered how this was going to work out.

She was glad she had decided eventually to dress formally. It was bad enough to be facing this nightmare, without arriving in any way dishevelled. Obviously Jordan had come to the same conclusion, because as she opened the door his tight look vanished and he looked at her approvingly, his eyes running over the slim lines of her suit, the short, boxy jacket, the straight skirt.

'Splendid!' he pronounced. 'That rich blue looks good on you.' He glanced keenly at her. It was clear that she had slept badly and he frowned slightly, his lips tightening again. 'Everything is going to be all right, Cassy,' he said briskly, picking up her suitcase and standing back for her to precede him. 'In a few hours you'll be wondering what all this worry was about.'

She didn't think so, but it was nice to have someone to share the worry. She was also more than a little uptight about this trip with him. He appeared to be unconcerned that he was openly calling for her, that they were both away from the *Herald* on the same day. They were both well known in the town, and she had this feeling that many eyes watched their departure. Jordan Reece didn't seem to have any feelings about it at all.

She could have relaxed as they left the town had this been any sort of normal visit, but as it was her moodiness grew as they travelled, and after a while he turned to her with a look that was pure exasperation.

'While realising that this is a very personal nightmare to you,' he said tersely, 'I do feel that you should remember that when we get down there you will be expected to pass certain tests, the very least of which will be the ability to talk to me. Nobody, least of all someone like Lavinia Preston, is going to believe in this engagement if we look at each other blankly and refuse to speak!'

'I'm sorry.' Cassy looked at him a trifle mutinously. 'I know it's true, but I can't think of a thing to say. After all, it's not as if we're friends, or even like each other a little. This is just not going to work,' she ended, with a sigh that annoyed him even more.

'It's not going to work if we don't work on it!' he rasped. 'For the weekend at least we'll have to put aside our mutual irritation and get to know each other.'

'And what about the rest of the time?' Cassy asked, annoyance in her voice at his attitude. 'What about these—months that we'll have to keep it up for your father?'

'We won't have to keep it up under his nose!' he assured her testily. 'We both work, and luckily we both work a long way away. We can have another quick rehearsal if any other visits are necessary.'

'Well, of course they'll be necessary!' Cassy retorted sharply. 'I'll want to see him when he gets out, visit him in hospital, see that he's all right and . . .'

'Pity that you're not able to pretend you're engaged to my father when you meet your ex-lover!' Jordan grated. 'You've shown more enthusiasm speaking about him than about the whole of this mission.'

'Luigi isn't my ex anything!' Cassy snapped angrily, irritated at his tone. 'And naturally I'm comfortable speaking about your father; I know him. I don't know you at all. Until last night, you've done nothing but growl at me. I was never scared to go into your father's office.'

'You're scared to come in now that it's mine?' he asked with a tone to his voice that might have been surprise, but might equally well have been satisfaction.

'Yes! If you must know, then yes!' Cassy exclaimed, turning to him furiously, her mahogany-coloured curls swinging wildly.

He glanced across at her quickly, his silver eyes flaring over her rosy cheeks, her angry brown eyes. Then he looked back steadfastly to the road, and when she glanced at him, a little worried about her outburst, his lips were twitching in amusement.

'Sparky, aren't you?' he remarked softly. She didn't answer, and he reached across to take her clenched fingers in his warm, strong hand. 'Count to ten and we'll re-start,' he suggested quietly. 'Let's begin with the premise that you and I are engaged. Let's get acquainted. I don't want any awkward questions that we can't answer. I'll begin. I'm thirty-six, I was born in London, I'm named after my maternal grandfather. I went to an ordinary grammar school where I was expected to work like hell, and I then went to Cambridge. The rest, I told you—roughly. I never talk about my—adventures.'

'You don't need to, I've read your books,' Cassy murmured, and he looked across in surprise.

'Have you honestly? I'm flattered, unless you thought they were dreadful?'

'No, they were good. A trifle sad...' she added thoughtfully.

'Life's like that,' he assured her grimly. 'Now it's your turn,' he added on a determinedly bright note.

'This is a bit silly,' Cassy said, blushing and looking down at her hands. 'I feel as if we're playing games while the tumbrels roll.'

'It's not that bad!' he laughed. 'Just remember, though, that your mother will be suspicious. My father won't, he'll be delighted!'

'You're cold-blooded, aren't you?' Cassy said tightly, and he laughed again, a hard, harsh sound.

'You already know that, don't you? It doesn't extend to my father and mother, though, just everyone else.'

'Oh! I don't know much about your mother!' Cassy said with a gasp of dismay. 'Only her name!'

'Dorothy,' Jordan said in a satisfied voice. 'Dot, to my father. What did I tell you? Get on with your life history. I can't perform well if I'm going to have to turn to you every other sentence and say "I didn't know that, darling". Your mother is going to wonder what we do with our time!'

Cassy went a startling shade of pink, glad that he didn't seem to notice, but she took his point now and began to talk. He was a good listener, and after a while the embarrassment died and she had no idea that the loneliness of her girlhood came through clearly.

She was surprised when he turned off to actually enter London, and couldn't help pointing out that this would waste a lot of time.

'Probably so,' he murmured, his eyes on the fast traffic, 'but don't forget, we're engaged, and as yet you're not wearing a ring.'

'It's not at all necessary,' Cassy got out hastily, a deep anxiety growing out of nowhere that had nothing at all to do with meeting her mother and Luigi. 'Lots of people nowadays...'

'I'm not lots of people!' he said briskly. 'My mother and father are old-fashioned, they'll expect it. You're mother is rich, she'll be looking to see approximately how much the ring cost. Left to you, I can see that this trip would be a fiasco. Your mother would tell us to learn our lines and try again next audition!'

'Well, you've passed a lot of jewellers,' Cassy said impatiently, unspeakably anxious now about having Jordan's ring on her finger, even though it was all make-believe.

'I have a special place,' he said determinedly.

'I see. You usually get your engagement rings from the one jeweller's, then?'

'Tut!' he said ironically. 'You'll have to be less abrasive if this engagement is to be believed. As a matter of fact, I bought a watch here for myself, the first time ever that I felt anything approaching solvent. I had my first month's salary from television, and I went overboard and bought an expensive watch.'

'That one?' Cassy asked, looking at the thin gold watch that adorned his strong wrist, wondering if she should try to get into television if they paid so well.

'No,' he laughed, 'this came with fame. The other is saved for posterity. It was a thrill at the time, though,' he added softly.

'But now you're all grown up,' Cassy murmured, looking with misgivings at the glitter in the window of the jewellers where he stopped his car.

'Yes,' he said briefly, 'grown up and cynical.'

Nerves silenced her once they were inside and he was greeted with smiles and obvious recognition, his name rolling off the tongue of the assistant with ease. The manager appeared like a grinning genie within minutes.

'Fame, not notoriety,' Jordan murmured at her scathing look, and then her looks were only anxious as trays of glittering rings were displayed for her to see. Of course, she could not choose. It was ridiculous and rather underhand to be choosing a ring merely to deceive his father—about her mother she had no such misgivings—and in the end Jordan chose. It was a diamond cluster, the central diamond large and beautiful, the whole thing heavy and frightening on her finger.

It gave her an odd feeling, as if she was dreaming, and she had to pull herself sharply back to the present as she realised that the manager was watching her with the rather tender look of one who had seen it all before and that Jordan was asking her opinion.

'Do you like it, darling?' he said quietly, and she muttered that it was very nice, the manager's sigh of contentment embarrassing her into wild blushes.

'She'll keep it on,' Jordan announced firmly, taking the box and handing it to Cassy as he got out his chequebook. The price frightened her into further silence, and she muttered furiously to him as they left the shop.

'I'm not at all sure that you're sane. A piece of costume jewellery would have done. Nobody knows the real thing any more.'

'Oh, you innocent child!' he taunted. 'Someone like your mother could distinguish between a fake and the real thing at fifty yards. In any case, frightening I may be, irritating I most certainly am, cheap I am not! And just to prove it, guess where we're going for lunch?'

'I never said you were frightening,' Cassy insisted, her eyes on the glitter of the ring, the weight of it on her finger somehow irritatingly reassuring. 'I said I was frightened to come into your office!'

'In future, I'll summon you and then shout from the next room,' he assured her. He glanced down at the ring and then at her awe-stricken face. 'Sparky, like you!' he said firmly.

They went to one of the most expensive hotels for lunch, and Cassy was thrown into another small panic at that.

'Why are you doing things like this?' she asked in an agitated voice, stopping in the doorway. 'I—this suit is...'

'You look very nice,' he said quietly, standing quite still, not coming for her but waiting for her to go to him. 'The colour is quite startling with that hair.' She went forward and he took her arm in a firm grip. 'The skirt is a successful length, too!'

'It's perfectly normal,' Cassy muttered. 'Skirts are shorter now.'

'Really?' he murmured. 'I was beginning to think that perhaps legs were longer!'

It did nothing to make her feel easy in her mind, and they knew him too—again!

'The price of fame,' he said dismissively. 'Surely you've been out with your mother?'

'Not that I remember,' Cassy said shortly, uncomfortably sure that she had offended him in some way when she looked up and saw a deep frown on his face. They were talking, though, that at least was a step forward; and then there was the ring, glittering on her finger like a charm to ward off evil. Surely with this she would have no need to act? Surely her mother would be completely taken in? She hoped so, because she knew now that, without Jordan there, she would never have managed to get through this weekend.

It was months since she had been down here, she realised, as the Porsche climbed the hill to the village. Her father had been so remote, so utterly indifferent that she had left sooner than she had intended, and her heartbeats quickened when Jordan turned his car to the left at her instruction and the house came into view.

It was not a beautiful house, it was big, white and quite imposing, the gardens reaching to the road, and Jordan stopped at the wide, white gate, pulling up behind a huge Daimler, her mother's normal form of transport.

'They're here already,' Cassy said in a frightened voice, every bit of confidence draining away as she saw again the car, the white house, the past.

'Play this my way,' Jordan said quietly. 'I want you to go up there alone, just ahead of me, and I want you to remember that you're not a young girl any more, that a good deal of time has passed. You don't live here any more, either. If it gets too much we simply go—call this a flying visit.'

Cassy looked at him anxiously, but he nodded firmly to the path, quite determined, dominant.

'Go on,' he ordered. 'Just open the door and walk in, I'll be not too far behind. I'm the surprise, the ace up your sleeve. We play the ace carefully!'

She went, although her legs were trembling. Sometimes now she could not remember Luigi's face, sometimes she totally forgot, smiled and enjoyed herself, but she knew why she shunned people, had become wary of men, and deep down she knew that she could be hurt again very easily.

She could hear them as she went into the hall; at least, she could hear her mother's beautiful voice and that seductive, gurgling laughter. Perhaps Luigi was not there? Perhaps this was not some cruel, pointed reminder? She opened the door and his was the first face she saw.

He was sitting by the fireplace, glass in hand, laughing at something her mother had said and Cassy's breath almost stopped. He was just the same. His hair was black, slightly wavy, thick and gleaming. His eyes were dark and liquid, and as he saw her the smile died on his face for one telling second before he stood and drew the attention of the other two to the fact that their daughter had come home.

'Cassandra, you managed it! And so early, too. You must have made an enormous effort to get here so soon. It's lovely to know that you wanted to see us so very much!'

Her mother came forward, her green eyes sparkling but so watchful, so carefully ignoring Luigi Rosato and the fact that he stood stock still, his eyes intently on Cassy's face. And then the ace played itself. Jordan walked into the room, bringing the whole thing to a halt as his arm came firmly around Cassy.

'You left your bag behind again, darling,' he said amusedly, his lips brushing her hair. 'It's getting to be a habit.'

She jumped, but he covered for her quickly, putting her bag into her hands, drawing her firmly to his side, his height making her feel tiny. It was quite frightening to have his arm around her. She had never felt at ease with him, and there was an awful trapped feeling as the strong arm circled her waist. It was a long time since any man had put his arms around her or even touched her at all, and she was almost holding her breath, willing him to let her go.

'Jordan! Jordan Reece!' Her mother stopped and looked at him in astonishment. 'You came with

Cassandra?' Clearly she thought it impossible, and equally clearly she knew him. Cassy stiffened further, but his arm tightened warningly around her.

'Well, I would want a few explanations if she came with anyone else,' Jordan said easily. 'I tend to get a bit annoyed if any man comes within half a mile of her, except my father of course, who adores her.' He swung Cassy towards him with what seemed to be the ease of long practice. 'My sweet idiot, are you going to tell me that they don't know? Haven't you even written to tell your parents that we're engaged?' His voice was warmly amused, but his eyes were cool, turned from the others and harshly warning.

'I—I've been so busy...' Cassy murmured, her face flaring with soft colour. She had never known her mother to be silent for so long, and when she turned back it was to see a very strange expression on her mother's face, an expression she could not in any way read.

'You're engaged—to Jordan...?' She seemed stunned and Cassy's nerve came back with a rush as Jordan's arm tightened painfully.

'Obviously!' she said with a laugh, holding out her hand, the ring glittering expensively. For once in her life, if only for a moment, she had the upper hand here and she felt an unexpected sense of companionship with her domineering, cool boss.

'So that's why you're so early? You came to tell us...'

'Not particularly,' Jordan murmured amusedly, his hand ruffling Cassy's hair playfully. 'Some of us thought you knew!' He smiled into Cassy's eyes, apparently pleased with her performance, and then turned back to her mother. 'As a matter of fact, we simply took the day off. We don't often get a long weekend.'

It was all too much for Lavinia, she was being upstaged. She took over, her bewildered look vanishing as she urged them into the room.

'Well, don't just stand there, come in!' She turned to Giles Preston, who was looking at Cassy with equally startled eyes. 'Darling, they're *engaged*—you must have champagne somewhere. Get it out!'

Without Jordan she could not have managed; Cassy told herself that over and over again. He was subtle, playing his part easily, not too possessive, not too close, just the faint suggestion of complete oneness with her that was very convincing. Her father brightened up, the most cheerful she had seen him in ages, and Jordan talked easily to all of them, obviously relaxed and assured.

'Of course, Cassy probably mentioned Luigi to you?' Lavinia said in an offhand voice as they sat. 'She knew him when she was at college.'

'Why, yes. Let me see, you're an actor?' Jordan said with a brief smile in Luigi's direction.

'Oh, he's going to be really good one day!' Lavinia said hastily, patting Luigi's hand. 'After all, he's learning from me. One of these days his name will be in lights. I haven't seen you in ages, Jordan,' she went on, covering the sudden uncomfortable silence. 'It was when we had dinner at the Carlton, wasn't it?'

'Yes,' Jordan agreed wryly, 'and the whole place was in an uproar, everybody on their feet, clapping!'

'But they recognised you, too!' she gurgled happily. 'You're quite a celebrity yourself.'

'Not any more,' he said evenly. 'I've gone into relative seclusion. I'm running the group of papers my father set up.'

'How incredibly dull for you!' Lavinia said in a shocked voice. 'So dreary after all that excitement, you must be bored.'

'Not while Cassy's around,' Jordan said promptly, his arm coming casually around her shoulders. 'And speaking of being around, I'm afraid I can't let you have her for the whole weekend. We're going to my home, too. Tonight and half tomorrow is all you get. That's why we came early.'

Cassy realised that Luigi was sitting quite still, watching her. So far she had avoided his eyes, too afraid to look at him, but Jordan had now thrown her in at the deep end, and if she was to stay here tonight he would have to be faced.

She looked up and met his steady gaze, her smile as genuine as she could make it. The dark eyes held her with the old familiar ease, making her heart sink. What would she do if he touched her? Would she give the whole game away?

'You have grown even more beautiful, Cassy,' he said quietly. 'You are not quite as I remember you, though. You look finer, different.'

'Why, Luigi, I'm astonished and flattered that you remember me at all,' Cassy managed. 'I was thinking on the way here that I could hardly remember your face.'

'But you were thinking about me?' he said with a soft laugh. 'At least that is something.'

She felt Jordan stiffen, his hand tightening on her shoulder, and it gave her the courage to reply with a light-hearted ease. 'Of course I was thinking about you. Mother is here and so obviously you would be here, too. I tend to bracket you together in my mind, like salt and pepper, bread and butter.'

'Darling, I'll get your suitcase,' Jordan said, rising abruptly, just as Giles Preston reached again for the champagne. 'I'll have to go, then. I'll be back later.'

'What about another glass?' her father asked, a smile on his face that surprised Cassy.

'Just one,' Jordan said pleasantly, 'and then I really must be off.' He raised his glass as soon as they were all served. 'To my future wife!' he said clearly, and Cassy felt a shiver run over her as their eyes met. There was a tone to his voice that worried her almost as much as all this elaborate farce, but he hadn't finished yet. He looked at Lavinia and added quietly, 'And to my future mother-in-law!'

She took it very well; after all, she was an accomplished actress, one of the best, but there was a slight flush on the beautiful cheeks and her smile was just a trifle glassy. Being a mother-in-law was just a little ageing. Somehow, Cassy knew that she wasn't going to take this lying down.

She hurried after Jordan as he went to the car, speaking anxiously and a little crossly when the others were well out of earshot.

'Where are you going, for heaven's sake? You're leaving me!'

'There's no need to panic,' he assured her quietly. 'I'm going to book myself in at that big hotel just at the end of the village. I can't face a long time with Luigi, he's really not my type at all. In the meantime, you can talk to him and to your mother, rub your father up the right way and unpack the things you need. Tonight I'll take you all out to dinner, tomorrow afternoon we whistle and ride!'

'You know her, don't you?' Cassy accused quietly, a little surprised at the disappointment she felt about the fact he had not spoken of it. 'You never told me that. You had dinner with her.'

'And about ten other people,' Jordan said calmly, lifting her case out. 'We were on a chat show together, everyone went to dinner later. That is the extent of my knowledge of your mother, apart from seeing her perform twice and what I read in the papers. Your body language is quite explicit at the moment,' he added softly. 'You are aggressive, uptight, clearly quarrelling with me.'

He put the suitcase down and cupped her face in his strong hands.

'We have an audience,' he informed her as she stiffened. 'Your mother is smiling suspiciously at the door and your ex is at the window.'

'He's not my anything!' she began angrily, and he looked steadily at her, his fingers lacing into her hair.

'He appears to be unsure of that. Let's convince him,' he said determinedly. He pulled her forward into his arms, speaking against her hair. 'I'm afraid that a stage kiss will not do, Cassy,' he murmured. 'The great actress would spot it easily. It's got to be the real thing, sorry!'

His head came down slowly, his silver-grey eyes holding her startled gaze, and his lips lightly brushed hers.

'Just relax,' he murmured against her lips, 'honestly, it's not going to hurt one tiny bit.'

Nobody had kissed her since Luigi. The thought flashed into her mind as his lips waited over hers and panic shot through her, an unnatural and frightening desire to break free and run, to fight wildly, to escape from revulsion. And somehow he knew it. His arms tightened, making any move impossible, his hand cupped her head and the hovering lips swooped down to claim hers.

At first she didn't know what was happening to her. A curious feeling hit her inside, a feeling oddly like excitement, and she knew it must be anger, bottled-in rage. She went stiff, but he merely deepened the kiss until she felt breathless, and she relaxed as ordered when a peculiar peace seemed to enter her whole body.

Instantly he lifted his head, his eyes sardonic and cool.

'My, you're difficult!' he said tauntingly. 'I'm only supposed to be half of this act, remember? So far I've been the leading man, the clown, the stage manager and just about every other damned thing. If Lavinia believed that, she must be getting old!'

'It wasn't necessary!' Cassy snapped, her face flushed and angry, her feelings back to normal with a rush as his glittering eyes surveyed her flushed face with something close to contempt.

'Any more trouble from you and I'll take off without you tomorrow,' he threatened, his dark brows raised.

'You wouldn't!' she gasped, panic returning as anger faded.

'I just might,' he warned with clear satisfaction at her return to supplication. He put her case just inside the gate. 'It's not heavy. You can play the role of porter. If I come up there I'll have to kiss you again, and you'll probably break out in a rash! See you in about an hour,' he said briskly. 'Tell them that your betrothed is taking them out to dine.'

He drove off, leaving her staring after him, quite sure now that the turmoil inside really was fury.

Luigi was there almost at once, lifting the suitcase and taking it to the house as she walked unwillingly beside him.

'You have quarrelled with him?' he asked quietly. 'Is this why he leaves you to bring the suitcase inside?'

'Of course not,' Cassy said with a light laugh. 'Jordan and I never quarrel.' She felt that she should have her fingers crossed at this lie, but Luigi took it at face value. There was a shaken feeling inside her now that Jordan had gone, and she wished him back here with a fervency that surprised her.

'He is a powerful man, not the sort of person I would have thought to see you with at all. I remember your preference for gentle people. There is nothing gentle about that man.'

'Don't be ridiculous!' Cassy snapped, irritated by his reminiscences and by a strange loyalty that she suddenly felt for Jordan Reece. She had enough problems without taking on guilt; after all, this was a mutual arrangement, even though the role Jordan had to play was harder than hers.

'You knew me a very long time ago,' she reminded him sharply. 'My tastes in things and in people have changed a great deal. I'm a very different person now.'

'I do not think so,' he said quietly. 'To me you are still the same—beautiful, tall and slender, the same rich, glowing hair.' He put the case at her door, apparently remembering the room that had always been hers. 'I feel the same exactly, *cara*,' he said deeply.

For a moment their eyes met and Cassy was swept into the darkness of them, the smile of them. Memory came with a rush and she was back in Luigi's arms, hearing their shared laughter, remembering the sheer joy of being with him.

Her mother called from the stairs and the smile died from his eyes, a faint glint of anger glittering somewhere at the back of the dark glow. He did not move, but Cassy did. Before he could intervene she picked up the case and went into her room, closing the door and leaning against it as her breath left her in a shuddering sigh.

Luigi still had the power to call to her without words, the ability to hurt her badly. She was suddenly fiercely glad that Jordan was here, that his strength would stand between her and this situation. Tonight she would show them, all of them, that she really was engaged to someone as hard and dynamic as Jordan Reece. He was quite right, she hadn't been trying at all.

When she went downstairs her father was alone, and he shrugged when she asked where the other two were.

'Walking round the garden, I believe,' he told her offhandedly. 'I think your arrival and the unexpected sight of that huge ring has created some sort of crisis.'

Cassy looked up quickly, and caught a wry look on his face that she hadn't seen for years.

'Don't you care, Daddy?' she asked quietly, coming out with something she had never said before. 'She's your wife.'

'And you're my daughter,' he said evenly, looking her in the eye, his indifference for once not uppermost. 'Theatre people are supposed to be very emotional, you know, but personally I think it's all show. We use our emotions too much in front of the footlights to have many left. There are a few, though, and I've never been so filled with satisfaction as when you came here today with Jordan Reece. He's more the man for you than that doe-eyed Italian. You're not at all like your mother, Cassandra. You need someone to look after you, someone to take your hand and take responsibility for you. You've got the right man, my dear. Don't start yearning for something that would have been the biggest mistake of your life.'

He picked up his newspaper, apparently quite satisfied that the discussion had ended.

'Daddy,' Cassy said impatiently, sitting at his feet and pulling the paper away. 'I was talking about Mother, about you, both of you!'

'I know Vinnie!' he said, laughing suddenly as he added, 'She doesn't like to be called that. I used to call her that when we were first married, but she's too important now. Cassandra, she has done what she liked all her life. She's a star! Do you know that even this house is hers? I've never even tried to compete, not even when we were young. When this Italian palls, she'll drop him from a great height. I've seen it all before.'

'I don't understand you,' Cassy said softly.

'Don't try, my dear,' he advised quietly, 'concentrate on Jordan, not that I imagine he'll allow you to concentrate on anyone else,' he added with a grin, ruffling her hair; it reminded her how Jordan had done that. She was beginning to think he would be better on the stage, too; his acting ability was tremendous.

Her mother walked in at that moment and stopped dramatically in the doorway, Luigi looking a trifle awkward just behind her.

'Well, well!' she said with obvious amusement. 'I'll have to get here more often if you two are getting so cosy. What plots are you hatching, darlings?'

'Not plots, character discussions—other people's characters,' her father said cynically, and Lavinia Preston's green eyes were suddenly cold and thoughtful. At that moment Cassy felt a sudden wave of pity for Luigi. He was just not in her mother's class. Why she had collected him was a mystery, except for the very obvious reason. It disgusted Cassy all over again, and words after that came easily. She spent the whole time wilfully talking about Jordan, aided and abetted by her father who, to her great relief and even greater surprise, had also read Jordan's books.

CHAPTER FOUR

WHEN Cassy saw the inside of the hotel where Jordan had booked, she was grateful yet again for his foresight. Of course, her mother had been astonished that Jordan wanted to stay at the hotel instead of the house, but he had waved her prying aside easily.

'This is Cassy's day, her home,' he said, smiling down at Cassy as she nestled unwillingly against his arm, having been pulled there relentlessly as soon as he came back to the house. 'I understand that you don't see much of each other. It will give you time to have a good talk without me around. She can tell you my good points.'

It was a very clever dig at her mother as far as Cassy could see, but Lavinia gave one of her rueful smiles and passed it off easily, as only she could. Luigi had been very attentive, his dark eyes angry as he watched Jordan's possessive arm around Cassy, and it had not been at all difficult to blush and look flustered with so many watchful eyes on them.

This was different, though. The hotel was big. It was also popular, especially on Fridays when there was a dinner-dance, and Jordan had booked a table at the side of the room, manoeuvring Cassy to the seat by the wall, securely trapped at his side and well sheltered from her mother and Luigi. It had all been done so skilfully, her father placed opposite, and if she had not been so suddenly and inexplicably attuned to his actions Cassy would never have noticed. Nobody else seemed to realise that they had been carefully placed like pieces on a board-game.

He took over most of the conversation, too, and she was beginning to imagine that she would get away scot-free when Luigi suddenly asked her to dance.

'Oh, I . . .' Panic immediately flared inside Cassy and her mother pounced as if she had been waiting for this.

'Oh, go on, Cassandra!' she urged teasingly. 'You've got to come out of that corner some time. You danced so well with Luigi when you came home for the summer vacation. Do you remember? It's just like old times.'

Yes. That was when he had told her he intended to go with her mother to New York. That was when he had asked her to wait, to let him have his chance. There had only been the one dance, after that her mother had been the only one his eyes saw. Cassy slid out as Jordan held her chair, and she felt that she was living the past all over again.

She had to steel herself to go into Luigi's arms, and she was almost sure that he knew it. He tightened his arms around her and for one moment she was back where she had been so long ago: happy, sure, the lazy, dark eyes making love to her. She had been here before too, in this place, on this dance-floor, in these arms, her mother watching.

She stiffened and pulled sharply back, glancing up angrily to see amusement in the dark, glowing eyes.

'When you came home today, when you came into the room, I knew that you remembered,' he said softly. 'When he came in behind you, I could not believe it. We were always meant for each other, *cara*, you know that. Why are you doing this to us?'

'I wonder if you're drunk?' Cassy said coldly. 'I'm engaged to Jordan, and as to "us", I haven't the slightest idea what you mean. It was a long time ago. I was very young and very foolish. You were older and able to lead me in any direction you chose. I grew up, face it!'

'He is as old as I,' Luigi said with a smile, apparently not believing anything she said. He was astonishingly sure of his own importance. Cassy had never noticed that before. 'He is wrong for you, *cara*. He is so wrong that I am suspicious. Are you really engaged to such a cold man, a man with eyes like icy seas?'

They weren't! When Jordan laughed his eyes were warm, glittering and compelling. Cassy suddenly realised that, and realised too that any hold on her that Luigi had in the past was now broken. Her worries and doubts were all so much sentimentality. He was merely annoying her and making her feel very treacherous as he talked about Jordan. She discovered with a shock that she knew Jordan Reece much better than she knew Luigi. She had never known anything about Luigi at all, and now he was a complete stranger who was very good at irritating her.

She pulled completely away, turning towards the table, and he had to follow whether he liked it or not. Jordan's eyes were glacial as he watched, and she wondered if she should have stuck it out. What was he thinking?

'What a short dance, darling,' Lavinia said, her voice bubbling with quite malicious laughter. 'Are you tired?'

'Only when someone steps on my toe twice!' Cassy said briefly, moving to her place as Jordan stood.

'Come along,' he said coolly. 'I'll try to make up for it.'

Cassy didn't have much choice, she was out on the floor before she could think of any excuse.

'What was that all about?' Jordan asked curtly. 'You were in his arms, out of them and back in again like a yo-yo!'

'I'd no idea we had such an attentive audience!' Cassy snapped. 'As a matter of fact, I had to get away from him fast.'

'Before you melted completely?' he asked witheringly, and she glared up at him, astonished as ever to notice that even with high heels she only came to his chin.

'It's none of your business!' Cassy snapped, angry at being taunted when she had been thinking so loyally of him before.

'Then shall we let them into the secret?' he asked coldly. 'Shall we walk over, toss the ring on the table and shout "April fool"? Why bother to carry on with this if we're no longer on the same side?'

'It's just that you annoy me,' Cassy told him quietly, getting her temper back with a rush at this threat. 'You seem to make me say things I never intended to say. I was angry with Luigi because he suspects and said so.'

'What exactly does he suspect?' Jordan asked calmly, and once again she felt sheer exasperation at this cool, powerful man who took every last thing in his stride.

'He suspects that we're not really engaged!' she snapped. 'I suppose this is all a complete bore to you, not at all tricky after your exciting life, but I'm finding it very difficult to side-step the remarks I'm getting. Only Daddy seems to be taken in. Those two don't believe it at all. They're probably watching us quarrel right now and muttering in agreement that this is a very clear farce.'

'Finished raging?' he asked quietly, his deep, calm voice stunning her, making her look up at him quite startled. 'If you have, then we'll do a little convincing, but I warn you, Cassandra, I'm fed up of being both the horse and the cart. Co-operate or we'll pack this in!'

He pulled her close in his arms, much closer than Luigi had done, and if the others at the table thought they had been quarrelling, they could now see clearly that the quarrel was at an end. His hand came to her hair, stroking through it before gently pulling her head to his shoulder, and Cassy played along, well aware of the eyes that would be watching, assessing. She only had to let Jordan lead.

He opened his jacket, placing her hand against the steady beat of his heart, his lips brushing her cheek as she looked up at him hastily.

'Stay there, Cassy, my darling,' he murmured softly, and she immediately obeyed, worried that her legs were trembling and that something altogether odd was happening to her.

'Why did you say that?' she gasped, turning her suddenly hot face against his chest.

'I read somewhere that your mother can lip-read,' he murmured against her hair, laughter at the back of his voice. 'It's not unusual for actors to be able to do that. I'm taking no chances.'

'I'm sorry about all this,' Cassy confessed with a little sigh that was shaken in spite of her attempt to stay as calm as Jordan. 'I realise that you've done more than your fair share. I'm just in a complete panic all the time. I've got to face it all over again at your house, too.'

'It's going to be different there, Cassy,' he murmured. 'My parents will be falling over themselves to believe it. I can quite see why you were so upset before. Apart from a certain glee at the back of your father's eyes, you're facing a good deal of hostility here.'

'That's nothing new,' she sighed. 'I've always had to watch my step, and I always knew that mother didn't want me around much. A daughter is particularly ageing to an actress; people begin to compare, to add up years. I'm quite surprised that she ever owned me at all.'

'Poor little devil,' Jordan said softly, but she heard the laughter at the back of his voice and her head shot up from its safe resting place, her brown eyes instantly angry.

'I'm not anxious to have pity!' she snapped, stiffening in the strong arms. 'Just for a moment there I simply forgot who you were.'

'*They'll* be wondering who I am if you keep rearing up to fight,' he assured her, his voice filled with derision. 'You've just undone the good work I've achieved since we began to dance. Now I'll have to start all over again.'

She felt his lips on her cheek, moving closer to her mouth, and she knew she would have to co-operate this time. He was not going to keep on threatening. She turned for his kiss and his mouth closed over hers as he pulled her back to him. She had been ready for it this time, willing to co-operate, but she had never expected to co-operate so well.

His mouth suddenly hardened to possessiveness, the kiss deepening, and shock-waves of feeling hit her deep inside, making her lips part involuntarily. It was the sudden heat that shot through her, a feeling somewhere on the edge of beautiful, but frighteningly strong, and Jordan took instant advantage of her weakness, his tongue invading the tender warmth of her mouth as he stopped pretending to dance at all and concentrated on the kiss.

Cassy became aware that he had lifted his head reluctantly, that the music had stopped and that they were the centre of many pairs of amused eyes. Colour flooded into her face and Jordan turned her back to the table, his arm tightly around her waist.

'Well, if that doesn't convince them,' he murmured, 'nothing will!'

He released her and took her trembling hand, holding it warmly, his thumb brushing encouragingly across her wrist.

'Keep looking just like that,' he whispered as they neared the table. 'You're doing just fine. I forgive you your previous slips.'

How he could be so cool, Cassy had no idea. If she didn't sit soon, she would fall in a heap at his feet!

'Jordan, really!' Lavinia looked unusually shocked, her laughter a very thin veil covering disapproval. 'I'm not sure that you're safe to be left alone with my daughter.'

'Ah!' Jordan looked casually across at her, his smile edged with mockery. 'Cassy is now about to step completely into another life. Your hold on her is very weakened.' He put Cassy's hand on the table, keeping it in his own powerful fingers, but turning it so that the glittering stone caught the light. 'My ring! Cassy is now mine, Lavinia. I'm not used to stepping aside from anything, and I'll never step aside from Cassy.'

A great wave of alarm raced through Cassy at the cool, determined words. Did he have to commit them so deeply? What about the time when the engagement would end? Lavinia would never stop laughing!

She glanced up at him in a sudden panic, but the strange, compelling eyes held hers and the firm lips smiled with barely hidden mockery before they brushed hers possessively. She was very glad after all that Jordan was staying here at the hotel; a few more remarks like that and they would both be trapped so tightly that this engagement would have to go on for years instead of months!

Cassy felt utterly worn out the next afternoon as they drove towards Surrey and Jordan's home. She was quite lifeless and she knew it. Jordan had collected her, and after one sharp look at her pale and weary face he had said nothing at all. She was grateful. She needed no words, too many of them had already been spoken.

The night before she had been unusually lucky. Jordan had seemed unwilling to let them go. He had talked easily to her father, danced with her mother and taken most of the strain from Cassy. This morning, though, things had caught up with her.

Luigi had followed her around with a sort of desperation, his conversation returning again and again to the engagement, and when he had finally managed to corner her alone he had pulled her roughly into his arms.

'I cannot let you step out of my life, Cassy!' he said urgently. 'When you came yesterday I was waiting to ask you to marry me, to come back to New York with us when we went.'

'Are you mad?' Cassy gasped, a brilliant flare of relief flooding through her as she realised that she felt not the slightest pulling at her heart-strings at this assertion. 'For four years you've been with my mother! What sort of a fool do you take me for? I no longer care a damn what you do, Luigi. Just get the idea firmly fixed into your head that I'm happily engaged, and stop talking like that right now.'

'I cannot stop,' he said heatedly. 'You have become hard with this man, but it does not matter at all. Stay here and let him go. Give back that ridiculously expensive ring!'

She had thought herself that it was ridiculously expensive, but when Luigi said it she suddenly saw red. It was nothing to do with him! He was a stranger and Jordan was . . . was . . . She found herself stopping, her mind racing with unusual feelings. The annoying, irritating man who had made her life a misery had become during the course of three days a tower of strength, someone who shared her secrets, someone to run to. It stunned her, and Luigi mistook her suddenly still expression for something entirely different.

'Cara!' He pulled her back into his arms, but for a second only. As Cassy reacted with a feeling akin to violence, her mother appeared and Luigi strode off angrily.

'People who step out of their depth usually sink,' Lavinia said warningly, her green eyes sharply on Cassy's bewildered face. 'You are the limit, Cassandra! You can't handle Luigi, who is the most painfully obvious wretch. How do you imagine you'll ever manage a real man like Jordan Reece?'

'What Jordan and I do is nothing to do with you at all,' Cassy said sharply, no fears or worries left in her, her mind almost totally given up to her own private puzzling about her new attitude to Jordan.

Lavinia put a cigarette in the long, expensive holder, her movements sharp and annoyed.

'Jordan Reece is too old for you,' she said impatiently. 'Good heavens, there are even flecks of grey in that thick, dark hair. He's probably older than Luigi, and he's fifty times more difficult to handle.'

'I prefer older men,' Cassy said with an unusual burst of spite. 'Daddy knows me far better than you do; of course, that's only natural, I've always seen more of him. I could never settle for someone twelve years younger, I'd feel like his aunt!'

'What you don't know would fill an encyclopaedia!' Lavinia snapped, colour flaring unpleasantly over her cheeks. 'You'll not get the sort of marriage you expect with Jordan Reece. He's too tough for you. I'm more the type to handle him.'

'Let's not talk about the type you are,' Cassy snapped back as she walked out of the room.

She remembered her pain, her disbelieving misery when this had all happened before. Her mother had handled Luigi so easily, hooking him and reeling him in with a smile of triumph. Jordan was not led anywhere. Jordan was strong and determined, coolly aloof. She was utterly confident that if her mother tried any of her tricks with Jordan they would be met with smiling disdain, or even harsh reproof. She couldn't wait for him to get here.

As they left, her father shook hands with Jordan vigorously, his own personal triumph gleaming in his eyes that slid with amused appraisal to Luigi's tight face. Her mother kissed Cassy's cheek coldly and then turned to Jordan with a smile that was all seductive charm.

'In all the surprise, I've never really greeted you as one of the family, Jordan,' she exclaimed, coming forward with the clear intention of kissing him, and Cassy tensed visibly, embarrassment and anger flooding over her.

Jordan coped, of course, turning the tables easily. He took her mother's hand, not even kissing it, bowing over it with a courtly dignity.

'We'll have to come to some arrangement when Cassy and I are married,' he murmured mockingly. 'Will I still call you Lavinia, or will you expect to be called Mother?'

It was a reproof delivered with smooth ease, and it was the final line. For a second even Lavinia Preston's superb acting ability faltered. She laughed delightedly, but Cassy saw the sharp burst of anger at the back of the lovely eyes and she was glad to put her hand in Jordan's as they left the house together.

'Hungry? I know I came a little early and dragged you away before lunch, but there's still a way to go. Do you want to stop for lunch now?' Jordan's deep, quiet voice pulled her back to the present, and Cassy smiled a little wanly.

'Yes, please.' She sighed deeply and sat up resignedly, her eyes avoiding his face. 'Thank you for coming early and—and for everything.'

'I was anxious to get you away,' he said briskly. 'There's a lot of unseemly emotion running around there.'

She felt as if that was a reproof for her, too, and her embarrassment held her silent. There was a lot of unseemly emotion. There was her own, or at least, there had been. Someone like Jordan would have simply sent them a 'drop dead' message, or gone to laugh at them, or even ignored the whole thing.

There was her mother, too. It was not just this morning that she had launched herself at Jordan. In the hotel last night she had played the seductress fairly openly. If this engagement had been real, Cassy would have been frightened that history would repeat itself. To Jordan, it must all be a little sordid.

'Don't forget, you'll now get the chance to continue your act,' he said softly when she simply sat in uncomfortable silence. 'This time, though, I can promise that there'll be no sniping at you. You're going to see someone who really cares about you, so from this moment you can relax!'

'I hope my conscience doesn't smite me too hard,' Cassy murmured. 'I'm really fond of your father, too.'

'Oddly enough, so am I!' he said testily. 'I also have a conscience. I have to weigh up one thing against another. I imagined that we'd both done that and come up with the best solution for *his* benefit.'

'I know. I—I'm sorry,' Cassy said a little miserably, and he glanced across at her sharply, a slashing, silvery appraisal.

'Shake off those idiots at your house, Cassandra, or I'll pull over and shake you!' he said sharply. 'My father expects to find you normal, sparky and insubordinate. If you're submissive, I'll get the blame.'

He turned into the forecourt of a hotel and stopped.

'Perfect timing,' he murmured, glancing at his watch. 'We'll eat here.' He got out and strode round to her door, reaching in to help her out determinedly, so determinedly that she swayed, almost off balance, and his arm came around her to steady her at once.

'You'll have to walk in by yourself, I'm afraid,' he told her amusedly. 'You have to be a bride to get carried over any threshold!'

She blushed to the roots of her hair and glared at him.

'Good. Back to normal!' he jeered softly. 'It's fairly easy to wind you up.'

Cassy looked at him reproachfully, suddenly not feeling so comfortable with him any more, and he took her arm, his expression softened as he turned her towards the hotel and lunch.

'Come on,' he said gently. 'It's all over. The rest will be a pleasure.'

He laughed softly at her deep and tragic sigh, and the feeling of comfort came back with a rush, the tension leaving her shoulders as he urged her into the hotel, his hand warm against her back.

'Well, there's one thing,' Cassy said thankfully and a trifle thoughtlessly as they ate lunch in the warm, cosy dining-room of the hotel, 'with your father and mother we'll not need to act out our engagement so vigorously!'

'I'm not sure that's an advantage,' he confided with a low laugh. 'There's a certain spice about kissing someone who resents you. It's an incredibly easy way of putting the female in her place.'

'That's a very typical chauvinistic attitude!' Cassy snapped angrily. 'That's the unacceptable male attitude in a nutshell. Sex as a weapon.'

His wide grin showed her just how very easily he could wind her up, make her dance to his tune, and she glared at him openly.

'To hear you use the word "sex" is astonishing,' he goaded softly. 'It sends an odd shiver down my spine, you being a hard-bitten newshound, self-sufficient and man-hating.'

'I'm none of those things!' Cassy exclaimed in growing annoyance, adding with malicious enjoyment, 'My mother seems to think that you're much too old to be engaged to me.'

'Now that's just not true,' he assured her, even more amused. 'Whoever marries you finally will have to be prepared to teach you a lot; your faults are endless. You have a bad temper, questionable manners, a stubborn nature and an absurd ability to suddenly melt into very feminine tears. A younger man just could not cope!'

'Have you quite finished?' Cassy asked, enraged.

'You want more?' Jordan enquired, his eyes alight with mocking amusement.

'Oh, shut up!' Cassy snapped. How she could have thought him comfortable, she did not know. It was ridiculous; she knew perfectly well what he was like—hadn't she worked with him for long enough?

She was still simmering as they left and he was still amused. She sat stiffly in the car as he got in and fastened his seat-belt.

'Well, that's quite restored you to normal,' he said in a smug voice. 'Watch out when we get back to the office. I've really learned how to handle you now.'

'Is that why you said all those things?' she demanded angrily. 'To return me to normal after being at home?'

'Why else?' he asked softly. His hand reached out and tilted her face. 'Do you think I want to hurt you,

Cassandra? You seem to me to have been hurt enough already. You're still hurting.'

She stared at him for a second, her eyes puzzled, and he let her go, starting the car and driving off. She wasn't hurting. She realised that with a great surge of joy. This weekend had cured something that had been lingering like a disease. The liquid, dark Italian eyes were no longer a weight at the edge of her heart. The eyes she saw were grey, silver-grey, determined and all male, very irritating, a little too masterful, but always oddly comforting. They saw her fear, her pain, her need as well as her temper and stubborn nature. The only thing wrong was that Jordan Reece was far too dangerous to ever be called a friend.

She laughed aloud as she saw the house where Harold Reece lived. It was long and low, surrounded by a garden that she realised would look lovely in the spring and summer. But the thing that brought forth laughter was the fact that a river ran close to the house at the back.

'I might have known!' she exclaimed delightedly as Jordan turned questioning eyes on her. 'Harold Reece without a fishing-rod in his hand is quite unimaginable, really.'

'He looks more normal in his fishing togs than at any other time,' Jordan agreed with a smile. 'My childhood memories are weekends spent beside rivers, my mother reading or knitting as my father tried to teach me the finer points of catching the wily trout.'

It silenced Cassy. Her memories were of nannies who left as soon as she was used to them because her mother found endless faults with them. Her memories were of a silent house as her mother and father left for weeks away at different theatres. There were times when she too was drawn into the theatre world, sitting entranced in the atmosphere of glitter and greasepaint, but those times became rare as she got older and her mother found it difficult to reconcile her own youthful appearance with Cassy's growing beauty and long-legged elegance.

Surely Jordan was normal and steady? How could he be otherwise with a normal home and a father like Harold Reece?

'Regretting it, Cassy?' Jordan said a little tightly as they got out of the car.

'No.' Cassy shook her head and looked at him a trifle wistfully. 'I suppose I'm just envying you this—this normality and warmth.'

'Just step into it, then,' he said quietly. 'I can assure you that you'll be welcome.' His arm came round her waist as the door opened, their arrival noted. 'Someone in there cares about you, Cassy,' Jordan added softly. 'Just enjoy being spoiled for once; my mother excels in that field, I'll have to fend her off but there's no need for you to do that.' He looked down at her with a smile. 'Enjoy yourself and let the other visit fade out of your mind.'

She looked up into those compelling eyes, seeing reassurance and strength, and she suddenly found herself smiling. He looked pleased at that, and to her astonishment his lips brushed hers quickly.

'Here we go again,' he mocked softly as he turned her to the door and the woman who stood beaming at them, her eyes beginning to gleam with very obvious hope.

CHAPTER FIVE

DOROTHY REECE was quite small. The fact startled Cassy, but the smile in her eyes made up for any smallness of stature. She watched their approach as they came along the garden path, and her face was filled with such gladness that Cassy felt quite humble and incredibly guilty.

'Jordan!' His mother stood on tiptoe for his kiss and laughed up at him mischievously. 'We knew you were bringing Miss Preston, and I suppose from your father's descriptions that this is the one and only Cassy?' She smiled at Cassy, and then looked back at her son. 'Can we assume...? Unless you make a habit of kissing the features editor as a matter of course...'

Jordan laughed down at her and took Cassy's hand, displaying the ring.

'We're engaged,' he assured her, keeping Cassy's hand in his own, 'and don't go letting her know your opinion of me, please!'

'Oh, Jordan, I can't tell you how... Your father will be so thrilled! Oh, do come in, both of you!'

She darted inside like a bright little bird, and Jordan looked at Cassy with amused, warm eyes.

'Isn't she astonishing?' he said proudly. 'She's really doing very well. Normally she never finishes a sentence. I think she's being articulate for your benefit. She never stops talking and never finishes what she was going to say.'

'She's not at all like you,' Cassy whispered, the feeling growing in her that she should not be deceitful here with these people.

'I must have some of their good points, after all, surely?' Jordan said wryly. 'Keep a close watch and let me know later.' He urged her inside and she stiffened with fright.

'Oh, Jordan, I'm not sure that . . .'

'Let me down now,' he said tightly, his voice low and menacing, all laughter gone, 'and I'll really punish you!'

She didn't have time to reply because Harold Reece was suddenly there, his face so hopeful, so unbelievably glad and so pale that Cassy knew she would go through with this and keep it up as long as Jordan thought it necessary.

'Cassandra!' he said in a shaken voice. 'Dot says that you're engaged to this rogue. My dear, if it's true, then I'm the happiest man alive!'

'It's true,' Cassy said with a sudden tearful sound to her voice at the signs of his illness, her arms going out impulsively to hug him, although she had never done such a thing in her life before.

'And *I'm* the happiest man alive,' Jordan insisted as his father gathered Cassy into his arms and grinned happily at Jordan.

'You hard-bitten devil!' Harold Reece said affectionately, as they clasped each other in masculine embrace. 'How did you manage it?'

'I wore her down, didn't I, darling?' he asked with a wry look at Cassy, his temper restored at her greeting of his father.

'You could say that,' Cassy said tremulously, wondering why she was crying openly and they were just beaming at her.

'She suffers from a lot of feminine failings,' Jordan said softly, his arm coming round her. 'Did you know for example that she can cry at the drop of a hat?'

'Your father never made me cry,' Cassy managed tearfully, and Harold Reece let out a whoop of delight.

'Hah! That puts me ahead for some time to come,' he declared loudly. 'Did you hear that, Dot?'

'I expect to!'

Jordan's mother bustled in with a laden tray and Cassy was drawn into the warmth of this family, led to the long settee by Jordan and seated by a glowing fire, Jordan's arm coming around her at once.

'Unhand her, boy! Let her get a cup of tea,' Harold Reece ordered, sitting himself opposite and settling in to enjoy this visit, and Jordan released her with enough show of reluctance to make his mother's eyes grow dim with sentiment. 'Did you bring the week's papers?' Harold added sternly, and when Jordan told him that they were in the back of the car he dismissed newspapers at once, his eyes on Jordan's face.

'So, you're settling down at last,' he said with a great deal of satisfaction. 'Getting married and giving up this endless wandering into danger!'

'So it seems,' Jordan said slowly, his reluctant admission not lost on Cassy. He was suddenly stiff beside her and she felt an inexplicable sense of loss. He would never give up his life. He thrived on danger, challenge. His reluctance to state his aims was proof enough. Even he would not take easily to this kind of deception. His parents, though, seemed to notice nothing of this. They were too excited about the engagement, too thrilled by the present to question the future. She felt angry with Jordan for the way his father would finally be hurt.

'Are you going to book me into a hotel for the night?' she asked secretly when later they were left alone for a minute.

'Good lord, no!' Jordan exclaimed, looking at her as if she were mad. 'My father would take a club to me! You're expected here and you'll stay here.'

'I wish you'd told them about the—the engagement by phone,' Cassy said impatiently. 'All at once like this, it's a bit much for your father to cope with. He looks ill.'

'Of course he's ill!' Jordan said irascibly. 'That's the reason for all this, isn't it? Are you now blaming me for that? I left it as a surprise because I wasn't at all sure you would see this thing out, if you must know,' he added coldly. 'You've been wavering on the very edge of fleeing all the time.'

'I—I'm sorry,' Cassy said, bending her head, realising perfectly well what a burden he had found her to be. 'I know I've been difficult.'

'I expected you to be difficult,' he rasped. 'I also expected you to have courage. See that what courage you have lasts until we turn north tomorrow afternoon!'

She had asked for every hard word she got. She knew that, but even so his tone annoyed her and only the return of his father quelled the rebellion in her brown eyes.

It wasn't difficult to talk to his mother and father, providing the subject of the engagement and forthcoming marriage was left alone. This was a very different situation from the one she had faced at her own home. There, the battle had been to convince. Here, as Jordan had foreseen, no convincing was necessary. They wanted to discuss the future with a gleeful happiness that made Cassy wish herself miles away.

It was impossible to fail to be drawn into their warmth, though, and when Jordan suggested a stroll out of doors before darkness fell she was eager to go, wanting to give herself a break from the sheer guilt of her feelings.

'There's no need...' she began sharply as he took her hand and they stepped out for the nearby woods, both of them well wrapped against the cold.

'There's every need!' he answered angrily, maintaining his tight grip on her hand. 'My father's study overlooks this lane. Not for one minute will he be spying as your mother did, but he may well find it impossible not to peep a little and enjoy the fulfilment of his dreams! Destroy those dreams and...'

'There's no need to threaten me,' Cassy assured him sharply as they rounded the corner of the lane and were out of sight of the house. 'I care about him. I'm shocked at how ill he looks. If you think I would do anything to...'

'Then why are you so uptight, so reluctant to laugh and be normal?' he grated.

'I'm trying not to be too happy,' Cassy confessed bitterly, turning away. 'I'm trying not to be drawn into the warmth there, the love. I'm trying not to compare it with...'

'Oh, heavens, we constantly misunderstand each other.' Jordan stepped forward and reached for her, pulling her to him, although she came reluctantly. 'It's because we don't know each other at all,' he assured her, holding her close and stroking his hand through her hair. 'I'm completely to blame. I should have realised.'

'No, it's my fault. I'm behaving like an adolescent,' Cassy said unevenly. It was beginning to be altogether too comfortable when Jordan reached for her, but she made no attempt to move. She didn't want him to be angry again.

'Well, I did say that whoever married you would have plenty to teach you,' he quipped softly, 'but not this,

Cassy. You're very welcome here, you know that. Even if there had been no need whatever to pretend this engagement, you would still have been welcome. My father is very fond of you, and it's clear that my mother likes you, just for yourself.'

'I'm not altogether likeable,' Cassy murmured, and he tilted her face, smiling down at her.

'Sometimes you're quite likeable, oddly enough,' he said quietly. She went on looking into his eyes, finding something there that she had discovered a need for this past few days, and he let her go abruptly, turning her towards home after a few more minutes.

'It's too damned cold,' he said briskly. 'Let's go back.'

An odd disappointment washed over her, but she turned readily enough. It was cold, quite bitterly cold, and she was shivering.

'Your father was delighted that you'll not be going overseas into danger again,' she ventured quietly after a while.

'Yes. That's something that will have to be broken to him when he's quite well again,' Jordan said tersely, and Cassy bit her lip anxiously, wondering why this bit of information dismayed her so. After all, it was what she had expected.

Next morning she was awake early, curled up in the warm, comfortable bed in the old-fashioned bedroom when she heard stealthy steps pass her door. When she peered out, it was to see Jordan's mother in her dressing-gown, walking quietly towards the stairs.

'Oh, Cassy, I woke you up,' she whispered regretfully. 'I was awake and I couldn't wait any longer for a cup of tea.'

'Great! Wait for me.' Cassy darted back into her room, pulling on her dressing-gown and following Dorothy Reece downstairs.

It was warm and homely in the kitchen, the big Aga stove radiating a glow of comfort, and she remembered Jordan's suggestion that she should enjoy the love in this place, the warmth and homeliness.

'Ooh, lovely!' Cassy went near the stove and smiled across at Jordan's mother.

'Now, don't burn yourself, dear.' She bustled with the kettle and cups, and Cassy watched her, smiling.

Jordan walked in at that moment, looking big and alive, a white high-necked sweater and dark trousers making him look more powerful than ever.

'So this is what you get up to,' he said in amusement, 'A little hen-party. Dad's demanding tea,' he added to his mother, his grey eyes smiling at Cassy.

He looked a little overwhelming. The dark trousers hugged his lean hips, the white sweater stretched across his chest. He was amused to find her in her night attire, her long, curly hair in disarray from sleep, and she suddenly had to look away, her eyes going to the window and then widening with pleasure as she ran across the room.

'Jordan, it's snowing!'

'So it is.' He came up behind her as she stood, as excited as a child, and watched the falling snow; and this time she did not stiffen as his arms came around her waist. He pulled her back towards him and she came softly, aware that his mother was watching this little scene happily.

'Why do women get so excited about snow?' he asked teasingly. 'As a mere man, I think immediately that we'll have to leave early before the roads get too bad.'

'Oh, must we?' Cassy turned to look at him, and her disappointment made him laugh softly, his arms tightening around her as she continued to look up into smiling silver-grey eyes.

'I'm afraid so,' he said quietly, his lips brushing her cheek and lingering against the corner of her mouth.

'Harold will be furious,' his mother assured them. 'Here's your tea, however. I'll take his up to him.'

Jordan let Cassy go and walked across to the table to collect his tea, his eyes slanting a quick look at her.

'Well done,' he said drily. 'That was a really good bit of acting, soft and cuddly and all wide-eyed!'

Cassy took her cup and went upstairs to shower and dress, her heart beating much too quickly as she realised that she had not been acting at all.

They left after lunch, Harold Reece's disappointment persuading Jordan to stay after all, and although the snow was still falling the roads were clear. Cassy was silent, and there was no need to talk because Jordan seemed to be deep inside a gloom of his own—and she knew what it was. He had made what amounted to a promise to his father the day before, and he was trapped in it at the moment, the problem of getting out of it uppermost in his mind.

He took her to dinner when they eventually arrived back at Bradbury, but the meal too was silent and she was glad to get back to her own flat and solitude. She had a lot of questions to ask herself, many things to take out and examine closely, but the problem of her sudden and unexpected reaction to Jordan she left well alone.

Next day she was not too happy about the snow. It had been falling all night, and up here it was much deeper than the southern area. The weather forecast threatened more to come, and she felt as if she was starting a cold. When she went in to work her mind was not on things a bit, and she avoided looking at Jordan as he arrived and walked to his office. That was all over, finished. From now on there would be the odd visit to see his father, and then it would be ended completely.

'Hey!' Claud Ackland's whoop of sound as he passed her desk actually made her jump, but the annoyance in her eyes faded and turned to terrible embarrassment as he grabbed her hand and held it aloft.

'She's done it! Our Cass has actually done it. Look here, everybody!'

There was no way she could get out of this, even though she thought frantically, her cheeks flushed and her eyes wild. He held the hand up for all to see, and her engagement ring flashed almost blindingly. She had forgotten to take it off!

She was surrounded at once and her voice failed her as the questions flew at her from all directions.

'Who is it, Cassy?'

'Who's the lucky devil?'

'What a beautiful ring, it must have cost a fortune!' The women were more interested in the cost of the ring, but Claud Ackland was holding on to her hand and demanding explanations with a gleam in his eyes that was all news editor.

'Spill the beans, Cass,' he insisted firmly.

'I will.' The cool voice from just behind her made Cassy stiffen with fright. What would he say now? She had been stupid beyond words. She had been so pleased finally to have the ring, so secure in its comfort that she had simply forgotten that it was there.

'To take your questions one at a time,' Jordan said evenly. 'She's engaged to me, I'm the lucky devil and yes, the ring cost a fortune but it was well worth it to get Cassy.'

There was a stunned silence and Cassy's cheeks could blaze as much as they liked, everyone was looking at Jordan.

'Now,' he said comfortably, 'if we could get back to the business of producing a paper?' There was a flurry of activity and Jordan detained Claud Ackland. 'I think we should have the news first, Claud,' he said pleasantly. 'Get a picture of Cassy printed and sort one out of me. I'll give you the news in detail later.'

'Scoop!' Claud said gleefully. 'We'll have the TV people eating out of our hands for a day or two.'

'Keep them off my back,' Jordan warned. 'And keep Cassy well out of it.' His hand came to Cassy's arm. 'Cassy, I want a quiet word with you, please,' he said with deceptive gentleness, and she followed him to his office with more fear than she had ever felt.

'Jordan, I'm sorry. I'm terribly, terribly sorry!' she burst out as soon as the door was shut. 'I simply forgot to take it off. Oh, how are we going to get out of this?'

'Calm down.' He pulled out a chair and pushed her gently into it, walking round to sit in his own chair and tilt it back with his usual disregard for gravity. 'I had every intention of seeing you today to tell you that our engagement would have to be announced in the *Bradbury Herald*.'

'What?' Cassy sat bolt upright, and he grimaced and lowered his chair back to safety.

'Every weekend,' he said softly, 'I send my father the week's papers. He demands it. Don't imagine for one moment he's let the reins go entirely. What would he think if his own paper didn't announce the engagement of his son, the editor, and Cassandra Preston, the features editor? It's not even possible that in normal circumstances it would be kept quiet, everyone would know! Then there's your mother. She was not at all convinced, as you said yourself. She doesn't live on Mars, and she knows damned well where you work. Do you imagine she'll simply shrug and forget all about it? She'll snoop.' He watched her pale face and then said softly, 'It was inevitable, Cassy.'

'I'd never even thought about it,' Cassy said shakily, and he nodded, knowing apparently that she was given to bursts of stupidity.

'I realised that. I had thought about it, and as I said I was going to tell you, but as it happens it's all out of our hands and a damned good thing, too. It looks much more natural.'

'You—you're glad?' she asked in astonishment, and he nodded wryly.

'My dear Cassy, we've had one hell of a weekend! Do you think I like the idea of going through that regularly? It's just something that has to be done if the whole thing isn't to come thundering around our necks. Just let it be for a couple of days and everyone will stop being excited. Keep on smiling and blushing, refer all queries to me.'

She nodded a little numbly and stood to leave, anxious now to get out in case she had to face any ribald comments, but he stopped her as she reached the door.

'Are you all right, Cassy?' he asked quietly. 'You don't look too well.'

'Are you surprised?' she questioned weakly.

He frowned at her before grating, 'You looked pretty awful when I came in this morning. You don't look any better now. I asked if you were all right.'

'I—I'm fine,' she muttered, making her escape. A pretend engagement was not going to get her off the hook with him at work, that much was obvious.

There was an unusual silence in the office as she went back, but nobody said anything, not even Claud. He, apparently, was hugging his scoop to himself and didn't want to rock the boat in any way.

When lunchtime came, Cassy darted off rapidly and stayed out her full hour, although by the time she got back she was really cold and shivering. The snow was fairly deep now and some of the pavements were not as yet cleared.

'Let's hope they stir themselves,' Guy said as she stamped her boots free of snow, 'or we'll have another go at the council, this time about the roads and pavements. Are you all right, Cassy?'

'I think I've got a bit of a cold,' Cassy muttered, her voice rising to a surprised yelp as Jordan came in and grabbed her arm, almost frog-marching her to his office and slamming the door with complete disregard for the interested onlookers.

'Why the hell did you go off for lunch without me?' he demanded furiously. 'What sort of an engagement do you imagine they'll think this is?'

'I—did you expect me to...?'

'Engaged couples wish to be together!' he snapped, his voice filled with hostility and sarcasm. 'They *like* each other! When one races off and leaves the other behind, then people begin to speculate. As we've only just got engaged, this will be observed with great interest.'

Cassy's head was aching and she was shivering deep inside. She did not need this upbraiding, and she did not need biting sarcasm.

'This is not a normal engagement, and we do not *like* each other!' she raged in a quiet voice. 'I go for my lunch and I talk to people, I pick up news. You would be a drag.' She suddenly sneezed, the shock of it making her throat tighten painfully and her eyes run.

'You said you were all right,' he accused angrily as she buried herself in her handkerchief, and even then his voice was cold, domineering, superior.

'Go to hell!' Cassy said viciously and walked out. Half an hour later she really knew that she was ill and she spoke quietly to Guy.

'I feel really awful, Guy. I'm going home,' she told him. 'Cover for me, will you?'

'Sure.' He looked at her closely. 'I bet it's flu!' he said darkly.

'Don't sound so pleased about it.' Cassy laughed shakily, getting her coat and walking to the door. She was just at the bottom of the steps when Jordan caught her and marched her round to his car.

'Now I'm told by the deputy features editor that my fiancée is ill,' he snapped, pushing her inside the car and driving straight off. 'One of these days, Cassy...'

'Oh, do leave me alone,' she said miserably, and he grunted like an angry bear.

'With pleasure, once this is all over, Miss Preston. Until then, we're stuck with each other and I'd be very much obliged if you would remember that!'

When they reached her flat he came inside before she could stop him, and she began to fuss at once.

'What will people say?' she asked furiously, her head now so bad that she only wanted to crawl to her bed.

'They will say, "I always thought she was that sort of a girl," but later, they'll know that your betrothed was a truly thoughtful man who brought you home because you were ill. Get your things off and get into bed at once!' he rasped. 'I'll make you a hot drink and then I'll be on my way!'

For once she obeyed instantly, and when he knocked and came into her bedroom a few minutes later she was lying down with her eyes closed, the sheets almost to her ears.

'Are you still cold?' he asked quietly, and all she could do was nod; even that was painful.

He went out and she tried to sleep, the hot drink looking tempting but too much effort to reach. She was still awake and shivering when he came back into the flat, and a few minutes later he was in her room, a hot-water bottle in his hand.

'How did you get into the flat?' she muttered, but he simply ignored her and turned back the bedclothes, sliding the new hot-water bottle down to her feet and then tucking the bedding around her.

'Off to sleep,' he ordered. 'I'll get back to the office and look in on you later.'

'There's absolutely no need...' she began weakly, but once again he ignored her, and she heard the flat door close quietly as she snuggled down to the warmth, finally pulling the hot bottle close in her arms and falling asleep with it clutched to her.

She woke up later to find two people in her room, and one of them was Jordan. He spoke softly as soon as her eyes opened, his voice warning.

'Dr Jones, darling,' he said in what she imagined he thought was a soothing voice. It sounded perfectly menacing to her and she kept silent gladly, for more reasons than one. Her throat was hurting and her head threatened to leave her neck every time she moved.

She had her temperature taken and her pulse felt, and the doctor seemed to be fairly easy-going about it all.

'Just as I told you, Mr Reece,' he said mildly. 'Flu. There's a pretty virulent strain going round at the moment, and she'll be quite ill for a couple of days. Better keep her in bed for about three days and then let her up in the flat, but not outside by any means. Keep her warm and give her plenty to drink—soups, Bovril, things like that.'

Jordan was nodding seriously, and she wondered if they were both out of their minds. Jordan was not going to see to anything!

As soon as they left the room she got up, albeit with difficulty, and slipped into her dressing-gown. Here was where Jordan discovered that his role in her life was theatrical only. She staggered through to her small sitting-room and leaned in the doorway, unsure if she could get any further; then Jordan came from the front door, spotting her and looking at her furiously.

'What the hell...?' he began, but she stopped that straight away.

'Exactly what I was going to say,' she informed him in a trembling voice. 'What do you mean by coming here and taking over my affairs? I can cope very well alone and I don't want you here giving me soup, Bovril and "things like that"!' she added angrily.

'For once in your irritating life, you'll do precisely as you're told,' he snapped, sweeping her up into his arms and marching back to the bedroom. 'Fiancées like you are rare. Next time I choose one, I'll be extra specially careful. In the meantime, if anything happens to you, I will get the blame. Your colleagues will say that you were perfectly all right before you met me, which will be an utter lie, but it will be believed and my father will refuse to speak to me ever again.'

He threw back the bedding and slid her into bed.

'You will remain here and follow the doctor's instructions, and just to make sure of that, I will remain, too!'

'But you can't!' Cassy wailed, her hand to her aching head. 'People will...'

'The doctor will hear such rumours and tell them that you are quite ill and that only a lunatic would sleep with you. Your reputation is secure, Miss Preston, and when you're better you'll be quite pale and interesting—then we'll see!'

'What do you mean?' Cassy said anxiously, and he suddenly laughed, his hand soothing on her hot head.

'I'm making jokes to cheer myself up,' he confessed with a grin. 'Stay in bed, Cassy—please?'

She nodded, her eyes on his suddenly smiling face, and he went to the door.

'What—what are you going to do?' she asked anxiously, and he turned to look at her teasingly.

'I'm going to snoop around to see what you've got in the way of supplies, and then I'm going to the shops and coming back here to make a meal, something light for you and substantial for me. After that, I'm going to bed on your settee.'

'But you can't!' Cassy managed worriedly, knowing already that he could and he would.

'Being engaged is more of a responsibility than I imagined,' he said quietly. 'After this, I doubt if I'll try it again.'

He went out and, later, as she was drifting to sleep, she heard his car start and she knew that in spite of her protests he was going to do precisely as he liked. She felt too ill to care.

CHAPTER SIX

DURING the next three days Cassy was very ill, with little knowledge of what went on around her. She knew that Jordan was there, and that each day the doctor called, but the rest was really a bad dream. There was little sign of any cold, her head was too agonised to lift from the pillow except in times of sheer necessity. She was only vaguely aware that Jordan carried her to the bathroom, waiting outside to carry her back later, gently washing her face and hands and changing the crumpled sheets where she tossed fretfully each night.

It was Jordan who held her in his arms and carefully fed liquids into her, and it was Jordan who came in the night when she murmured in delirium, his cool, strong fingers holding her restless hands, his deep voice soothing.

On the morning of the fourth day she felt much better, and looked around at her familiar bedroom with eyes that were no longer aching. She felt very weak, but all the pain was gone, and she carefully made her own way to the bathroom, holding on to furniture as her legs threatened to give way beneath her.

He had promised that she would be pale and interesting, and she certainly was pale, her own appearance quite shocking her as she looked at her image in the bathroom mirror. She managed to get a reasonably good wash and she was just searching for a clean nightie when Jordan came into the bedroom, his face drawn and tired.

For a second he stood and looked at her, his eyes searching her face, and then he smiled wearily.

'How do you feel?' he asked quietly. 'I won't demand an explanation of this disobedience.'

'I feel shaken but mobile,' Cassy said weakly. 'I seem to have run out of nightwear,' she added in a puzzled voice.

'Ah, yes.' He ran his hand tiredly over his face. 'Jean will be here soon, she's been doing the laundry and a few small things for you.'

'Jean? From work?'

'The same,' he assured her. 'She offered her help. You've been very ill, Cassy. I thought that you might want a female nurse for some things. I imagined that you might be a little embarrassed afterwards if you discovered that I had changed your nightie, although she did mention with some amusement that you called her Jordan once or twice.'

He smiled suddenly at the look on her face, and walked determinedly towards her.

'Come on, back in to bed,' he ordered. 'You're still too ill to blush, and that's a very real sign that you should be safely tucked up for a while yet.'

'I seem to have caused a great deal of trouble,' Cassy murmured shakily as he helped her into bed, but he was busily wrapping her up and never met her eyes.

'As it was most certainly not deliberate,' he said quietly, 'I forgive you. The *Bradbury Herald*, however, is in an uproar. The features editor off, the editor and one reporter merely part-time as Jean and I take turns with our invalid. Guy is keeping everyone at arm's length in case he gets the flu, and the whole department is grinding to a halt.'

'Have you—did you...?'

'Sleep here?' he finished for her, clearly sensing her worry. 'Of course. Someone had to be with you. It was expected, so don't worry. Each morning as I've walked stiff-necked into work after a night on your none-too-comfortable settee, the only concern has been "How's Cassy?" No sneaky looks, no muttered comments. Your reputation is quite safe.' He sounded a little annoyed, and Cassy felt too weak to argue.

'As a matter of fact,' she said a little tearfully, 'I was thinking of your comfort and not my reputation. You're altogether too tall for that settee.'

'So I discovered,' he said with a rueful look at her downcast face. 'I'm sorry, Cassy. I seem to be a little short-tempered this morning.'

'I'll be quite all right to be left now,' Cassy said quietly. 'The flat's warm. I can go about carefully.'

'Tomorrow, perhaps,' Jordan said firmly. 'For now, I'll get you some breakfast and then I'll get over to my place for a shower and a change of clothes. Jean will be here about ten. Tonight we'll discuss the future treatment.'

Cassy found herself watching him with no idea why she did it, and he glanced up, his eyes meeting hers for a second before he suddenly walked out of the room.

Jean came in and brought the laundry, stayed to clean up the flat and gossip to Cassy, who felt as if she had been away for a very long time.

'There's chaos at the office,' Jean informed her. 'Jordan has hardly been there at all. I offered to stay here all the time, to sleep here too, but he wouldn't let me. He's spent the last three days simply ignoring the paper altogether. Claud Ackland has had to pull his weight at last; he's even stopped that annoying tendency to titter. Jordan hasn't taken very well to any sign of frivolity, he's been like a bear with a sore head.'

It filled Cassy with guilt. Jordan's belief that this engagement had to look real had certainly landed him with more than he had expected, and she had not forgotten his moody looks this morning.

She slept for a while after Jean had gone, and latcr made her way determinedly to the bathroom for a hasty shower before Jordan came back and refused to allow it. She was changed into a clean nightie and dressing-gown, just making herself a cup of tea when he came later. He had a huge bouquet of flowers in his hand, a bottle of wine under his arm and various supplies clutched to his chest as he wrestled with the door, and Cassy just stood looking at him with rather startled eyes.

He was so familiar now, so much the person she expected to look up and see, and she realised that she didn't want to see less of him. Somewhere along the line her feelings for him had changed; somewhere along the line she had become comfortable and secure with this hard and powerful man, and the knowledge stunned her.

He turned from the door and stopped abruptly at the sight of her standing there, his annoyed expression changing as he saw the look she was too late to hide.

'You don't follow orders too well, do you?' he asked softly, coming into the kitchen and putting his small burdens on the table. Cassy shook her head, too filled with troubled emotions at the moment to speak, and he looked at her quizzically before smiling down at her and handing her the flowers.

'Now that you're recovered sufficiently to notice, I've brought you these,' he said quietly.

She murmured her thanks, her eyes gladly turning to the flowers and away from him, and he took her arm firmly, heading her in the direction of the bedroom.

'If you keep out from underfoot,' he promised, 'I may well let you get up for dinner. Any sign of rebellion, however, and that privilege will be withdrawn.'

'I have to put the flowers in water,' she told him in a vague way, her mind not able to come to terms with her new feelings.

'Later.' He took them from her and opened her bedroom door. 'Be good, and good things will happen!' She looked up in surprise and he grinned unexpectedly. 'An old saying of my mother's,' he confided. 'It kept me in suspense and held any unruliness in check for days on end.'

'Did good things happen?' Cassy asked in a dazed sort of voice, looking up at him, feeling really small for the first time in her life, her height lessened by the fact that she was barefoot.

'Invariably,' he said firmly. 'My mother never cheats!'

She went disconsolately back to bed, his words ringing in her ears. *Her* mother cheated! Lavinia Preston fought for anything and everything she wanted, whether the loser was her daughter or not. Suddenly she found that the hurt had reorganised itself. She no longer cared what Luigi did, he had simply astonished and disgusted her. Beside Jordan he had seemed to be so much less than a man. The gentleness she thought had been there had now revealed itself to be merely weakness. There was gentleness in Jordan, too, but it was not weak. He was gentle with his mother and father, had been gentle with her when she'd needed it, but it had been the gentleness of the strong. How would Luigi have coped if she had been ill? Would he have looked after her and not given a damn what people thought?

No, that hurt had gone, the real hurt had surfaced, that her mother cared for her not at all, had never cared. The warmth in Dorothy Reece had never been in her own mother, and she herself had merely been a nuisance and a growing threat.

She was still sitting there staring at the wall, her thoughts dark and self-pitying when Jordan came into the room.

'The good things are now about to happen,' he began. 'I've actually made a fire in that small, evil fireplace and...' He stopped as he looked at her, and she realised with a shock that she was crying. 'Cassy?' he said softly. 'You should perhaps stay in bed, after all.'

'No.' She rubbed her eyes determinedly and swung her legs to the edge of the bed, reaching for her dressing-gown. 'I was absolutely wallowing in self-pity.'

'I see.' His face lost its concern. 'Luigi, I take it?'

'You take it wrongly.' Cassy informed him as she struggled to get into her robe. 'Luigi is an Italian wimp! I was crying for myself, not for him. I do recognise self-pity when I find it!'

'In that case you are allowed to eat in front of the fire,' Jordan said, with a return to humour. 'If you can make your way there, I'll bring a tray for you.'

'That was wonderful!' Cassy said later as she curled up in a chair and drank coffee. 'I feel as if I haven't eaten for days.'

'Which is more or less true,' Jordan remarked. 'As to the meal, I cheated. Most of it just needed heating. I'm especially good at reading labels.'

She found herself laughing, and he watched her with eyes that were filled with some deep consideration, his looks finally making her face flush softly.

'How is your father?' she asked quickly, preferring conversation to silence right now.

'All ready to go tomorrow,' Jordan said quietly, and she looked very startled. 'Tomorrow is Friday,' he reminded her. 'They want him in over the weekend for preparations. The operation is on Monday. You've lost quite a few days, Cassy,' he added softly.

'When will we go to see him?'

'Next weekend, if you're up to it,' he suggested. 'Right now you've a long way to go before you're well. The snow cleared, but more is forecast, so next week you stay in the flat and keep warm.'

'I'll be fine,' Cassy insisted. 'What about the paper? Other people are bound to go down with this.'

'The paper is coming out as usual, on time,' he said sternly. 'So far, Guy is still managing. Your feature has caused a spate of letters, nearly all in support. Guy is gleeful. You also missed the buzz that our engagement announcement started. Anyway, I've brought all the papers and you can catch up on the news tomorrow.'

'I'll read them tonight when you've gone,' Cassy said enthusiastically, and the dark brows lifted wryly.

'I'm going, am I?' he asked mockingly.

'I—well—I'm all right now,' she stammered, his clear, silvery eyes suddenly much too intent. 'Tomorrow I'll be back to normal almost, and then I can do everything myself. I'm really grateful but...'

'But your reputation is suddenly strangling you again?' he enquired sardonically. 'I shall be only too happy to sleep in a bed again, however. I can't say that any more nights on your settee thrill me. At one time I seriously considered taking you up to my house, but the thought of your reaction when health returned stopped that rather daring thought.'

Her rosy face seemed to amuse him greatly, but he relented after a second or two and turned to other things.

'One day next week, when you're feeling reasonably fit,' he told her, 'I want you to help me plan a Christmas party.'

'You're not going home for Christmas?' she asked in astonishment. 'What about your father and mother and what about...'

'Of course I'm going home for Christmas,' he said firmly. 'In fact, *we* are going home for Christmas!'

'I—I don't think that I...'

'You go to your own home for Christmas?' he asked quietly, and she shook her head, looking determinedly into the fire.

'No, I never do. Mostly my mother isn't there and my father goes up to friends in London. It—they always have. I mean, usually my mother has been away from England and—well...'

'You had Christmas with Nanny, I take it?' he asked steadily.

'Mostly,' she confessed, looking away from his suddenly thunderous face.

'You'll come with me!' he said in a voice that allowed for no dodging. 'Naturally you'll be expected. Dad will be recovering by then and there will be a steady stream of callers, from very odd relatives to very nice neighbours. That, however, is the real Christmas. This year I plan to set a precedent. I'm giving a party for staff and their wives and husbands a few days before Christmas. We'll get it planned!'

'I'd love to! Really I would,' Cassy said breathlessly, her eyes shining, and he looked across at her intently, his smile growing.

'I promised good things,' he reminded her softly. 'I wasn't quite sure how it would go down, though. It's going to be hard to reconcile this with your working image,' he added quietly. 'Right now, you look like a little girl. I'm surprised.'

'So am I,' she laughed. 'Normally I feel as tall as a horse. Sleeping on the settee has damaged your eyesight!'

'You can hardly be compared to a horse,' he said softly. 'A long-legged filly perhaps...'

He stood as her face suddenly flooded with colour, his eyes leaving her in peace as he looked around for his coat.

'If you're sure you can manage,' he said, 'I'll go to bed at my own house tonight.'

'I can manage,' Cassy assured him quickly, suddenly wanting her flat to herself so that she could search rapidly for her old self-assurance and a safe footing in a suddenly worrying situation.

'Then you can see me out and lock up firmly,' he said as he shrugged into a thick sheepskin coat. 'Tomorrow I'll stay at work all day. Jean will call and then I'll come for dinner. I'll cook. It's quite easy when you buy it all in containers.'

'I can manage,' Cassy said again a little desperately, but she was still feeling too shaken to stand up to someone who towered over her. He shook his head firmly as he reached the door with Cassy one step behind him, anxious to lock him out.

'One last time!' he ordered. 'I shall arrive with containers, wine and suitable goodies. Make the most of being ill! It may never happen again.'

'All right,' she said a little shortly, and his dark brows shot up in mockery.

'You're so gracious, Miss Preston,' he informed her sardonically, and she looked hastily away, knowing perfectly well that she had deserved that. She had no idea how to behave with him, after all.

'I'm sorry, I didn't mean... I'm so grateful that...'

'Don't overdo it,' he warned amusedly. 'One sorry and a couple of tears are much more effective. Stop wandering around with nothing on your feet!' he suddenly added sharply. 'No wonder you're ill.'

Cassy looked up to tell him to mind his own business, but he was only laughing, and she had to admit that he could wind her up better than anyone she knew.

'Goodnight, Cassy,' he said quietly, a smile playing around his lips, and suddenly she had to smile too, until she realised that she didn't want him to go.

It must have been the expression on her face that made him pause as his hand came to the door, and he turned back reaching out and pulling her into the warmth of his open jacket, his hands on her shoulders as his head bent to hers. She found her face lifting quite naturally for a goodbye kiss, and he was gentle, almost tentative, his lips brushing hers before he lifted his head to look at her steadily.

Cassy never moved, and it was entirely her fault that he brought her back to him, his lips claiming hers again, searching and lingering, warm and thrilling. Her hands lay against his chest, her whole body submissive, and his hands freed the belt of her robe to slide inside and clasp the soft warmth of her in the cotton nightie, to pull her gently closer as the kiss deepened.

He was perfectly controlled, she knew that. Cassy was the one who saw stars, great fiery stars that raced around her and touched her lightly to send waves of pleasure through her from her toes to her fingertips. Her arms wound around his neck and he cradled her against him, kissing her face and neck, her eyes and her parted lips until she was helpless and trembling.

His face was serious when he drew back and looked down at her, his strong hands fastening her robe.

'That's the very last good thing for tonight,' he said softly. 'Lock the door, Cassy.' And he was gone before she had even begun to breathe properly again.

She locked the door quickly and almost fell on the settee as she returned to the sitting-room. What had got into her? Had the flu damaged her brain? If he had gone on kissing her she would have stayed there forever! She put her head against the settee arm, too shaken to move, but all she could think was that Jordan had slept here, and she shot up with such force that her headache came back swiftly. She would have to do something about this! She was beginning to feel differently about him—and one thing was quite sure: she would never, ever fall in love again!

Apparently she was over the attack of flu, because next day Cassy felt much better. Jean came and lingered, not really wanting to go back to the office and knowing quite well that Jordan would forgive any tardiness as she had helped out so much.

'Have you seen the papers for this week?' she asked as they sat with coffee after Jean had tidied and washed up. 'There was a lovely picture of you. Nobody knows when Patrick took it and I don't think Jordan had seen it before. He stared at it for a long time and then just marched off. I bet he was jealous,' she added hopefully.

'Jealous?' Cassy asked in surprise.

'Yes! You know—I bet he wondered how Patrick came to take it.'

She seemed to think it was sheer romance, and Cassy suddenly realised just how much subterfuge was going to be necessary at work. Almost from the moment that this engagement had become known, she had been out of things. Jordan had been the one to take the weight of it, but even that must have been easier without her there. There were so many small things that could arouse suspicion.

When Jean had gone, she went through the papers that Jordan had left for her, reading the features with satisfaction and then searching for the picture that had annoyed Jordan. It seemed quite ordinary to her, but she realised all at once just what it was that had made him walk off angrily, why Jean had mistaken it for jealousy. It was not her photograph at all, it was the two of them together, and the caption that headed the announcement went, 'Jordan Reece to settle permanently in Bradbury!' One thing was sure, Jordan had not given that headline to anyone. He had no intention of settling anywhere, and if they knew him as well as she knew him they would never have written it.

It gave her pause for thought. She did know him. Slowly but surely she had drawn close to him, and her attitude of a little while ago now seemed ridiculous. How could she ever have disliked Jordan? She suddenly felt much more easy in her mind. There was no reason why she should not enjoy this brief spell of engagement. It was to their mutual advantage, neither able to allow it to end very swiftly. There was no reason why they should not be friends.

She rang up the nearby grocers and did a little extravagant ordering of food, getting a promise of delivery within the next hour, and then, a little warily, she rang Jordan.

It was strange to be ringing her own office, and the receptionist recognised her voice at once, wanting to know how she was. It brightened Cassy up even more, and she heard the same romantic pleasure in the girl's voice that she had heard in Jean's when she asked for Jordan.

'Mr Reece? I have your fiancée on the line, sir.' The announcement almost shocked Cassy into putting the phone down, but Jordan was obviously amused.

'Hello, Cassy,' he said, and she could hear the laughter in his voice. 'I imagine that my fiancée is ringing me to say that the dinner is off?'

Normally, she would have been ringing for just that reason, and his knowledge of her character had Cassy's cheeks burning.

'Wrong, Mr Reece!' she said as lightly as she could manage. 'I'm ringing to tell you that you can forget the containers. I'm much better and I've nothing to do. I intend to reward you by cooking dinner tonight.'

She was quite pleased with that. It sounded very self-possessed and light-hearted.

'If you've been out . . .' he began, but she interrupted at once.

'I have not. The things will be delivered, so spare me a lecture.'

'All right, Cassy,' he laughed, 'I'll be there at seven-thirty.'

She looked at the clock when he had rung off, and thought what a long time it was until then, her lips catching between her teeth as she also realised that she was impatient to see him, to see those silvery eyes warm to match the sound of his voice. Perhaps it was not a good idea, after all? The thought of enjoying this brief spell of engagement now seemed a little dangerous, but she was stuck with it whether she behaved warmly or coldly to Jordan, and he had been so very good to her.

She made *blanquette de veau* and fruit simmered in syrup and brandy, then enveloped in small pancakes, and it took simply ages. She had only just finished and changed into her caftan when Jordan arrived, and he took one look at her pale face and then got very stern.

'I should never have let you do this,' he said worriedly. 'You're the most irritating female I've ever known!'

'It was no trouble at all,' she lied quickly. 'Anyway, I wanted to give you a thank-you meal.'

'A sort of last supper?' he asked wryly.

'And you said *I* was ungracious,' Cassy mocked.

His face lost its stern look and his lips quirked in the old way.

'I apologise,' he said amusedly. 'I give you permission to feed me. It smells good.'

He was all praise later, and Cassy's pale cheeks became flushed with pleasure.

'Where did you learn to cook like that?' he asked in surprise. 'I know it couldn't have been Lavinia.'

'No,' Cassy said quietly, a little of the pleasure dying away. 'As a matter of fact, it was a Swiss finishing school.'

Jordan just stared at her and she looked rapidly away. 'You're full of hidden talents, aren't you?'

And inhibitions, Cassy thought bitterly. Aloud she said, 'I'll make the coffee. My last act of gratitude!'

She was glad to get into the kitchen and away from those probing eyes. She was glad too to be able to take a steady breath. In there, with the fire blazing away, the cold outside and the warmth of the room, she had come dangerously close to wanting Jordan's arms around her. This madness seemed to have come from nowhere. She reached for the coffee-cups, looking down with little surprise to notice that her hands were trembling.

Something shot across the floor and Cassy reacted with astonishing speed, boosting herself on to the kitchen table, gathering her long skirts tightly around her and shouting 'Jordan!' in a strangled little voice all at one and the same time.

He was there like a rocket, stunned to see the position she had taken up, clearly expecting to see her scalded with hot coffee and not sitting with her knees under her chin in the middle of the table.

'Mouse!' she said anxiously, her finger pointing. 'Mouse!'

He began to laugh and it infuriated her. One of these days she was going to find a few men who were scared of mice and related vermin, and she was going to do a big double-page feature on them!

It seemed to Cassy that Jordan was merely sauntering, and the mouse was not going to sit quietly in that corner forever.

'It's there, look!' she pointed out furiously, not letting it out of her sight.

'I see it,' Jordan assured her. 'What I want now is a tin, preferably with a lid.'

'I have no desire to store it!' Cassy bit out. 'But in case you have a workable plan, there's an empty tin on the top shelf, complete with lid.'

'I aim to catch it,' Jordan said mildly, opening the tin and turning his attention to the unwelcome visitor.

'It's got shiny little eyes,' Cassy observed in a small voice. 'It looks scared.'

'Of course it's scared,' Jordan said scathingly. 'Considering the scare you gave me for my size and weight, it's a miracle it didn't keel over!'

She ignored the sarcasm.

'I don't want you to kill it!' she said urgently.

'Women have an annoying ability to be squeamish in several directions at once,' Jordan said disgustedly, and she snapped at him in irritation, her eyes still firmly fixed on the mouse.

'Mice are quick! They run up walls.'

'Doubtful,' he remarked, moving quietly towards the corner.

'They run up curtains!' Cassy snapped, certain that it would escape. 'They could equally run up clothes and—and things . . .'

'An alarming thought, I take your point,' Jordan said in a vague voice as his attention deepened on his quarry.

He suddenly moved like lightning and then slammed the lid on the tin.

'Want a close look?' he asked innocently, but Cassy drew her skirts even more tightly around her and shook her head vigorously.

When he came back from outside, she was still there, her eyes searching the kitchen steadily, inspecting every corner.

'I released it in your small front garden. No doubt it will find its way to some hole or other.' He stood at the sink with his back to her, washing his hands, turning his head to look at her after a second. 'It's gone. You can advance slowly now.'

'There may be others,' Cassy assured him, still searching around.

'A platoon of mice? Come now, is it likely?' He put the towel back and looked at her with amusement. 'You're a mixture of hard-headed clarity and fluffy nonsense!' he mused. 'Surely you're going to get that coffee and fulfil your obligations?'

Cassy slid carefully to the ground, and as she looked up he was standing close, grinning down at her.

'Go back to the sitting-room,' he said quietly. 'I'll make the coffee. You deserve to be looked after for a while after that superb meal, not to speak of the cabaret!'

For a minute Cassy frowned at him, but then her eyes began to sparkle and they were both laughing quietly.

'Go on!' His hands came to her shoulders and the smiles slowly died as they looked at each other for a long minute. She swayed forward and Jordan enfolded her in his arms, gently pushing her head to his chest, his hand soothing on her hair.

'Cassy,' he said deeply and slowly, 'you're a very—vulnerable person, starved of affection for years, hurt badly when affection was apparently given. You could so easily be at risk.'

Her cheeks flamed with shame and she pulled away, turning her back.

'The only weakness I have is that I've had flu and you've been kind to me. I'm grateful,' she said tightly. 'The gratitude is ended. Thank you for the timely reminder.'

She walked out of the room, tears of embarrassment swimming in her eyes. She knew full well what had happened. She didn't need Jordan to point out that last night and again now she had practically thrown herself at him!

He was right behind her as she walked to the settee, and he spun her round to face him.

'For pete's sake, Cassy,' he grated, 'I'm only human! You're beautiful, soft and warm. Do you think I don't want to hold you? Do you imagine I don't want to kiss you? Damn it, I *enjoy* playing at being engaged to you!'

Cassy couldn't face him, and he tilted her chin impatiently.

'Look at me. Are you going to avoid my eyes for ever because I tried to protect you?'

When she looked up, her eyes were swimming with tears, and he muttered angrily, pulling her into his arms, gazing down at her with eyes as silvery as stars.

'Suppose, just suppose that I can't stop?' he asked huskily. 'What then, Miss Preston? Do you really approve of office affairs? Do you want to come to your senses a few weeks from now and realise that the dislike you had of me was all too real and that this close feeling is a mixture of gratitude, relief and our own conspiracy?'

There was nothing soft and warm about Cassy now. She was right back where she had started, cold, stiff and wary, her face tight, with every feeling pushed well down.

Her mind wondering just how she had ever thought that she couldn't wait for Jordan to get here.

He watched her intently, his eyes narrowed, seeing her retreat into her shell, and he shook his head as he looked at her.

'Oh, no, you don't, Cassy!' he said tautly. 'You're not going back in there. I found out just what you are and who you are, and even if you hate me ten minutes from now, I'll not see you slip back into that old-maid future that your attitude will lead to!'

She had no need to sway towards him, he pulled her close swiftly, his mouth capturing hers when she tried to turn away, and he kissed her cold lips into life, ready when they opened beneath his, his hand gentle on her face as he explored her mouth slowly and deeply.

He pulled her to the settee, taking her back in his arms, trailing kisses over her cheeks, her eyes and neck, and she began to drift into a warm cloud, his voice only hazy.

'Relax, Cassy,' he murmured against her lips. 'You're lovely, warm, real...'

'Jordan!' She wanted to tell him that he could stop, that she had forgiven him for the sharp pain and shame his remarks had caused, but he refused to let her speak.

'Shh!' he whispered softly, his hands beginning to caress her, to move over her slowly. He moved the caftan from her shoulders, his lips running over her skin and the smooth rise of her breasts, and he was so gentle, so careful for such a strong, powerful man, that Cassy's bones seemed to turn to water and her head fell back as he kissed the line of her throat.

'Stay alive, beautiful Cassy,' he commanded. 'Stop hiding in there!'

She wound her arms around his neck and he crushed her tightly against him, kissing her deeply before letting her go. He stood and looked down at her.

'No, don't move!' he said sharply when she began to sit up. 'You look sultry and tempting lying there, the robe half off your shoulders. Lavinia is glossy, bright and beautiful, but you, Cassy, you're warm and lovely and you're real, all the way through. That was just a taste of loving, an appetiser. Don't step back now at all.'

He reached for his coat and Cassy managed to get her trembling lips to speak.

'I—I'll make that coffee,' she offered, wanting him to stay. 'I—I'm all right now.'

'Do you really think I am?' he asked quizzically, the corner of his mouth quirking. 'Don't you know why I'm getting the hell out of here?'

He stopped at the door and looked at her.

'We never did plan my Christmas party,' he said ruefully. 'Lock the door, Cassy, but this time—wait until I've gone!'

CHAPTER SEVEN

OVER the weekend Jordan didn't come, and Cassy accepted that he had a great deal more common sense than she had. If this engagement was to go on as it must, then the less they became involved with each other the better. The problem, of course, was that they both worked on the same paper and were under the eyes of people who were well used to being suspicious.

He rang her on Monday and there was that old, guarded tone to her voice at once.

'Cassy? How are you?'

He didn't say who he was, of course, he expected her to know at once. She did know, but it annoyed her that he imagined he would be the only man to ring her. He *was* the only man to ring her, she had long since frozen any others away, and her reaction was quite illogical as she knew perfectly well.

'Don't worry, I'll be back to work tomorrow,' she said shortly, and there was an exasperated silence from the other end.

'What I asked,' he said after a second, his voice back to coldness, 'was how you were, not where you were or where you intended to be tomorrow.'

'I'm quite better!' she snapped back. 'Obviously I thought that, as editor, you had a right to know when you're likely to get a member of your staff back.'

'So you're quite fit to go out, are you?' he rasped, no longer soft-voiced with her.

'Perfectly all right.' She could even hear the hostility in her voice, and she was dismayed that she had brought all this about. She wanted to go back to the beginning and start all over again, but it was too late. Once more she had been cold, ungracious and most certainly ungrateful. While she was thinking, he put the phone down and Cassy knew that she had put them right back where they had started, strangers with a secret that had to be kept. Now it would be all that much more difficult.

She was greeted like a lost soul returned when she went back the next day. Guy just collapsed in his chair and looked at her with relief.

'Now I can get some sleep at nights!' he assured her. 'You want bringing up to date, boss?'

'Later!' Cassy laughed. 'What I would like is for you to attend the morning conference until I know what's happening. At the moment I've got nothing to confer about.'

'You could confer with Jordan about what it was like when you were both cosily flu-bound in your flat!' Claud Ackland murmured in his snide way as he passed.

'Jordan gives all the news out about our engagement!' Cassy snapped at once. 'You're going in there, get it from him. I'll mention it to him later, though, if you'd rather, he might give out a Press release.'

Claud's face lost its speculating look smartly and Guy grinned all over his face.

'Cass is back to normal, man! Whatever did you expect?' he asked brightly. 'You know the rules. Fire a shot at Cass and then duck. It always ricochets!'

Cassy glanced up as Guy suddenly stifled his glee. Jordan was watching, cold-eyed. He could not have heard the whole thing, but he clearly had seen Claud's face and heard Guy's remarks. She looked down and avoided his eyes. What did it matter? Jordan already knew what she was like.

As they came back, Guy bent to speak quietly to her.

'Your beloved wants you in his office,' he muttered. 'You're not satisfying that man, Cass, he's back to glacial status. Give us a break?'

She felt she could do with a break herself. The last time she had been close to Jordan he had been kissing her, telling her she was warm and beautiful. The next time he saw her she had been reducing Claud to pulp. Her legs were a little weak as she walked quickly to his office and closed the door behind her.

'I won't ask how you are,' he said coldly. 'I can see you've everything completely under control and that Claud will have to get back behind the wire mesh! I imagine he was being insulting?'

'No more than usual,' she assured him coolly. 'Men like that are easy to handle.'

'Aren't we all?' he murmured sardonically, his eyes skimming her slenderness. She had lost a great deal of weight during her illness and it showed. She fully expected that he would tell her caustically she was all skin and bone, and her face flushed in anticipation. He surprised her, as usual.

'I thought you'd like to know how Dad is,' he said quietly. 'The operation was yesterday, if you remember? It was easier than they had anticipated, and he's comfortable. My mother saw him and she's happy enough.'

Cassy sat down abruptly, turning her face away, tears in her eyes at once.

'Oh, hell!' she groaned. 'I didn't remember!'

She searched frantically for a handkerchief and Jordan left her to it. She was so busy feeling sorry for herself, so busy blaming Jordan that he had not come back, although he had spent every minute with her when she was ill as if it was a real engagement, that she had forgotten the main reason for doing it in the first place.

'Stop that!' Jordan came round and pulled her to her feet. 'I didn't say that to make you feel guilty or to make you cry. Slacken off, Cassy. I was simply telling you something that I knew you would want to know.'

'I know,' she muttered. 'It's hardly your fault that I'm—I'm...'

'If you don't go out there soon,' he said sharply, 'Claud Ackland will be here with his nose under the door. He'll probably have a stop-watch on us from now on. Dry those tears. I couldn't care less if he thinks I'm making love to you, but I'm damned if I'll let him believe that I've been beating you!'

He was quite right, she had to get back out into the office; after all, she worked here and she could have expected nothing but sharpness at the way she had behaved.

'Where's your ring?' he suddenly snapped out, and she looked quickly at her left hand before sighing with relief.

'Oh, for a minute I thought I'd lost it! It's in my bag. I took it off this morning to...'

'Put it on and keep it on,' he said tightly. 'It's bad enough leaving here with tears in your eyes. Forget the ring and it's not going to be too long before we get very awkward questions. We end this arrangement when it's suitable for us, not when somebody embarrasses us into it.'

He too was right back to coldness and Cassy just walked out, there was little else she could do. They had not begun this as friends. They did not even like each other, and there was no reason for Jordan to change. He had been kind when she was ill, but even then it was only to keep up appearances. Why should he be anything but what he was when nobody was looking, especially now that she had led the way so well?

When it came to lunchtime she tightened her lips and walked to his office, going straight in as any real fiancée would have done and, of course, Claud was there. Shc might have known!

'Coming for lunch, Jordan?' she asked sweetly. He was not going to get the chance to rage about that again, but he barely glanced up.

'Sorry, I've got to hang on here. Can you manage without me?' he asked with only a vague amount of attention.

'Of course. I just didn't want you to be disappointed,' she said wryly, and that got his attention. Those silver eyes flashed sparks at her, but she smiled charmingly and went out alone. It would have been an uneasy lunch break if he had come, anyway. She looked up at the sky and realised that it was snowing again. History had better not repeat itself. This time he would let her die of pneumonia for sure.

With nothing to stop her she lost herself in work, going right back to her old ways, and it was a great relief not to have to worry about Jordan. By the time the day was over she was back into the swing of things, picking up all the threads and doing what she was paid to do, being the features editor. Once or twice Jordan came through, but when he spoke to her it was work only, one professional to another, and she replied in a like manner. He was putting on the pressure too, to such an extent that Claud apologised.

'Sorry about the earlier comments, Cass,' he said drily. 'I know now what you were doing at your flat when he was there. He was putting cold cloths on your head and making you type up copy!'

It caused a great laugh just as Jordan was leaving for an appointment, and he walked slowly over, his eyes on Cassy's laughing face.

'I won't be back again this afternoon,' he said, loud enough for everyone to hear. 'I'll meet you up at the flat and we'll get that planning done.'

'I—er... what time?' Cassy gasped, wondering where this was leading.

'Probably before you,' he said evenly. 'I've got my key.'

He bent and kissed her right in front of Claud's startled nose, and Cassy got the point at once. There were more ways than one of getting revenge. Unfortunately, she had to go on smiling.

Because Cassy and Jean were both back, the office was almost at full strength and the work done in good time so that, by five sharp, Cassy was back at her flat, greatly relieved to find that Jordan had not yet arrived. He probably had no intention of arriving. The remarks at the office were to keep her on her toes and to keep the others off the track.

He came almost at once, and made no comment about the fact that she was here at least half an hour before she should have been.

'If you could get a coat on,' he said briskly, 'we'll just get the shops before they close!'

'It's three weeks to Christmas. They all stay open until seven from now until Christmas Eve,' Cassy informed him, and he relaxed visibly, taking his own coat off and making for the kitchen.

'Good. You've got a little longer, then. After the shops, I'll take you for a meal.'

Cassy was a little irritated at the way he began to make tea as if he lived here, but she used the time to go and change into a soft woollen dress and get out her coat. She touched up her make-up and fastened her coat against the cold, finishing the preparations by putting on a fur hat. She was not going to get any sort of chill wherever Jordan wanted to go.

Normally she would have refused to go anywhere, but she knew perfectly well how she had behaved since yesterday, and she was still consumed with guilt that she had never asked about his father. They needed to be seen together, too; that was after all why he had invited her, and that was also why he had wanted her to help with his Christmas party.

He was standing in the kitchen, drinking tea, and he looked at her steadily.

'Want a cup?' he asked briefly, and she simply shook her head, standing there dutifully. He put his cup down and shrugged into his coat. 'Right, then. Let's go, comrade!'

Obviously he was amused at her Cossack hat, but Cassy ignored him. She wasn't going to ask what shopping he had in mind, either!

He was buying decorations for a tree, and after a few minutes of standing by stiffly, Cassy couldn't help but join in, gradually taking over as he seemed to hesitate. It was exciting. She never went to the effort of getting a tree now, and it was simply ages since she had handled the delicate baubles and bells that they bought. She cut in with orders of her own and Jordan left her to it, coming back with several boxes of Christmas crackers and paying for the lot.

They had an early dinner and then headed out of town, and that was when Cassy's nerve began to desert her and her spirits fall. For a little while she had been enjoying herself, quite forgetting that this was all part of the package of make-believe that Jordan was creating. There would be the party when she would have to stand by him and pretend it was all real. There would be Christmas with his parents—and then what? How long would they have to be close and go on pretending?

It would be better if they worked in different towns, on different newspapers. Obviously she would have to be the one to go, and she cast around in her mind as to where. It was not easy. The chance of a job on another evening paper would not come at once, but it would save embarrassment when this engagement ended. It might also give the impression that they were not getting along too well.

He had a house a few miles from town, and she remembered that his father used to live somewhere here. She had never been, though, and she recalled that Harold Reece spent only as much time here as was necessary. He had bought the house by the river a long time ago, and spent every spare minute there even before he retired. There was no river here.

Inside it was warm and beautifully furnished; when Jordan silently motioned her into the large comfortable sitting-room she was a little surprised to see that he had already bought a tree. It was huge, already planted firmly in a tub, and only a room of this size would have accommodated it.

'I see you believe in going for things in a big way,' Cassy remarked, not meaning to be sarcastic, but his stiff attitude did not soften and he clearly thought she was again in a fighting mood.

'With anything that interests me,' he grated. 'I now intend to decorate it. You can help if you like, or you can sit down and put your mind to the party.'

'I'd like to talk to you first,' Cassy said with a stalwart gathering of her courage. 'I think there's something we should discuss as soon as possible.'

'Very well.' He looked annoyed at the idea, but she was determined to get it out. 'Carry on.' He sat down, motioning her to a chair, and she plunged straight in before her nerve ran out.

'It's very tricky, both of us in the same office, having to keep up appearances, having to pretend that we like being together. I've been thinking that it would be better if we were working on different newspapers. That way we would be out of the spotlight and able to just pretend we were close. We could see your father at any weekend and we wouldn't need to bother being together at any other time. Obviously I'll have to be the one to leave, and I thought I would start looking for a new job almost at once.'

He just sat staring at her, and she had to steel herself to meet those cold, angry eyes.

'Is that the lot?' he asked in a hostile voice. 'That is the sum total of your machinations?'

'You can see the sense of it, surely?' Cassy said sharply, angered herself at his attitude.

'I can see the reaction of almost everyone if I allowed it to happen,' he bit out. 'I recall that you wanted the engagement to last for a day! I also recall that I explained to you the utter impossibility of anything of the sort, and I do not intend to re-state the reasons. Just for once, try thinking of this from another angle, from somebody else's angle. What do you imagine my father would assume? Or your mother? The office would be buzzing with rumour and speculation. If you're being seriously inconvenienced by being engaged to me on a temporary basis, then say so and we'll put an end to the whole thing. But I warn you, Cassy, you really would need another job then! When I was at home this weekend, my mother never stopped talking about you. She's taken to you as if you were her daughter, and I'll not have her hurt. Do anything to upset her when she's got worries about Dad, and I'll make your life a misery!'

Only one thing highlighted itself in her mind: 'When I was at home this weekend.'

'Did—did you go home?' she asked in a stunned voice, bewildered that she had not thought of that at all.

'Naturally. I went to see Dad before his operation and to give Mother a bit of moral support. Where the hell did you think I was? I couldn't take you, you were only just beginning to recover!'

She looked away, biting her lip, going over all the hard things she had thought. He had spent the better part of the week sleeping on her settee, looking after her, and then he had driven down to see his parents. And what had she done? She had been consumed with annoyance because he wasn't there. She had drawn up battlelines as of old, and all because she wanted him with her. Cassy sat silent, her own thoughts ringing in her head. She did want him with her! She just fought back every time she was hurt, and it hurt her when he wasn't there.

One day this arrangement would end, their conspiracy would be over and Jordan would go back to doing what he wanted to do at the first opportunity. It was not much use wanting him to be beside her, because this was just a make-believe time, as unreal and poignant as Christmas itself.

'Have you any other points to make?' Jordan asked impatiently, getting up from his chair and picking up the boxes they had brought in when she shook her head. 'Another crisis is passed, then?' he growled. 'Maybe now we can get on?'

Dazedly she stood and joined him. She found it hard to come to terms with her feelings for him. She had never intended to have any feelings for him at all, and already they were too well established to be pushed away. She began to put tinsel on the tree and he stopped, glancing at her curiously.

'Don't you want to get on with the planning?'

'We haven't all night,' she said quickly. 'I'll do the planning with no difficulty if you can just give me some idea of what you have in mind. I can do it at home or during a break at the office. No problem.'

'Ah, yes!' he mused. 'The Swiss finishing school. I forgot about that. You'll be able to give everything a sophisticated sparkle and I'll be able to take the credit! Keep doing the lower area,' he ordered. 'I'll get the step-ladder and start on top.'

She was glad when he left the room. It gave her a minute to collect her thoughts, but after much less than that time she decided to leave them where they were. She couldn't face them.

'This is a lovely room,' she remarked when he came back and propped the steps close to the tree.

'I thought you'd never say that,' he said with a slight smile. 'Every other woman who comes here raves about it!'

She was shocked into immobility for just two seconds. She had never even thought of Jordan with other women, and the feeling that raced across her skin at the idea was almost a pain. Why not, though? He was handsome, charming and intelligent. That he was with her and not with someone else was, as he had told her, because his father liked her best of all. It somehow underlined the brevity of their relationship, and she was silent. He wouldn't want any permanent relationship with anyone in any case. She couldn't see Jordan going off into dangerous situations and completely forgetting about the 'little wife'. His life had been disrupted by his father's retirement and ill health, but it wasn't forever. He would be telling himself that.

'Splendid!' Jordan came down the steps and stood back to look at the tree. 'I'll make us a coffee and then we'll have a ceremonial switching on of the lights!'

'There's this,' Cassy pointed out. 'I—we bought it for the top of the tree.'

She held up the five-pointed star and he nodded.

'OK. I'll pop that on before I switch on the lights. Coffee first!'

She walked around the tree as he left, looking at it from all angles. It was such a beauty. It looked lovely here in this warm room, with the thick beige carpet below it and the heavy curtains drawn against the cold evening. She didn't want to go. She would have liked this time to have been the one to sleep on the settee, Jordan's settee. She sighed, knowing perfectly well what was wrong with her but absolutely refusing to look at it closely. Anyway, she could put the star up; she could easily reach from the steps.

She climbed up and began to fix it, but it was awkward, the wires wrapping themselves around the branch before she had it properly positioned, and as she was leaning further to free it Jordan came back in.

'Cassy!' He put the coffee down and hurried forward, and until she spun round at the sharp sound of his voice she had been perfectly all right. Now she wobbled dangerously, trying frantically to reach the bottom of the steps before they went over and not succeeding at all. As she fell, Jordan caught her and the impetus landed them both on the floor, his arm shielding her head as the steps hit the thick carpet with a thud.

'Goodness!' Cassy looked up from her position on the floor and saw the tree from another beautiful angle. 'If they'd fallen that way, they would have ruined the tree!'

'They wouldn't have done us a lot of good if they'd fallen a few feet closer!' Jordan pointed out irritably. 'I might have known you'd be seeing to things. There isn't a thing that anyone can do that you don't feel able to do better, is there?'

She thought he was unnecessarily annoyed and looked up at him as he sat up and glared down at her.

'I was doing just fine until you came in, yelling,' she snapped, all the bewildering beauty fading. 'Next time you decide to have a party, get yourself a new fiancée!'

'Do you realise how foolish you look lying there on your back, blazing away at me?' He started to laugh softly and Cassy felt more annoyed than ever. She began to sit up but he pushed her back, his hand on her shoulder.

'Stay there,' he suggested in amusement. 'At least you're at a disadvantage in that position.'

She blushed wildly and his dark eyebrows rose.

'No innuendo intended, I do assure you!' he said sardonically. His eyes began to run over her, making her wish she had struggled and fought to get to her feet. 'The dress suits you. Unusual colour for you, wine-red, a few shades lighter than your hair. Miraculously, it works. You've got a flair for colour. Finishing school?'

'It must be my artistic talent struggling out,' Cassy said shortly, worried by the way he was looking at her and by the way she was beginning to feel. 'I must have inherited something from a theatrical family!' It sounded a little bitter and his eyes narrowed on her face.

'Luigi raising his head again?' he asked softly.

'Nothing is raising its head!' Cassy muttered. 'All I want to do is raise mine. Could I be allowed to get up now, please?' she added crossly.

'I don't think so.' He was above her, his hands at either side of her head. 'I believe I like to see you down there.'

It was the last thing she expected to hear, and colour flared in her face again as his eyes held hers.

'You're really scared, aren't you, Cassy?' he asked. 'Is that why you fight so much?'

'I—I'm not fighting,' Cassy said in a trembling voice.

'Don't, then,' he murmured, his head bending to hers. And then his lips were on hers with the same gentle curiosity, teasing and searching, slowly driving all her survival instincts into the background. She made an attempt to pull away, but it was only a token gesture. She wanted this, needed it, and Jordan seemed to know exactly what she needed. His fingers gently traced her face and the long line of her neck, and Cassy relaxed against him, warm and thrilled.

'That's it, Cassy,' he murmured. 'Come back to life. You've frozen up again without me.'

She suddenly realised what this was. No spontaneous act of lovemaking this, but a calm and planned session of softening up, for her benefit, not his. He needed this not at all. It was like a medical experiment.

She turned her head away, her eyes tightly closed, her throat tight too as she asked, 'Can I get up now please? Is the therapy over?'

There was a moment of stunned silence and then an almost tangible burst of anger and power that seemed to sweep right through him, almost lashing against her.

'You little bitch!' It was only a whisper of sound, but it was the most frightening sound that Cassy had ever heard. He was perfectly still, his hands no longer gentle on her face.

'Can I get up?' she asked with a little less determination.

'Damn you, look at me!' He gripped her chin, his fingers tight as he jerked her head up. She opened her eyes, looking at him, and she was afraid, afraid of the tension in him, afraid of the glittering silver of his eyes. She was wide-eyed with fear but he never seemed to notice that. This time she had driven Jordan Reece to a cold, primitive anger, and she was well aware of the quiet of the isolated house, the steady crackling of the fire the only sound to break the menacing silence.

'You think it was therapy?' he asked with soft hostility. 'If it was, it did not and never has worked. Perhaps you need shock treatment?'

'I don't need anything from you!' There was always defiance in her, she knew that, and there was a terrible need to fight her way out of this.

'Don't you?' The deceptively soft voice did not disguise his inner rage. 'What about the times you simply fell into my arms? What did you need then?'

'Not you! It was gratitude, and I was still not well. I dislike you and you know it! I may have needed you at the time we went to see my mother, but then again you certainly needed me. I'll stick this out for your father's sake, but I don't need any therapeutic kisses!'

He grabbed her shoulders, lifting her to him as if she were a mere child, his eyes blazing with fury.

'My last decision was shock treatment, remember?' he bit out.

His mouth clamped on hers in a fierce, ruthless kiss, forcing her head back and her lips open. She struggled and fought, but he was even stronger than she had imagined and her hands pushing against his chest were engaged in a futile battle that did not worry him at all. He never even felt it. He was too intent on punishment.

'No! Please!' Her voice was wild with panic, but it only seemed to drive him further. He pushed her to the floor, his weight subduing her, one powerful hand holding her wrists easily.

'You think you know me?' he ground out. 'You think I've set myself up to be your personal psychiatrist? You don't know me at all. This is how I am. This is how I am when my patience runs out!'

He bent to kiss her again, his fingers biting into her wrists, and she writhed beneath him, fighting with all her strength. But his mouth suddenly changed, clinging to hers as his personality seemed to change, too. One minute it was a fight, both of them bitter and angry, Jordan raging out of control. The next minute everything had changed, his whole body flared with passion, and he released her wrists to tangle his fingers in her hair and lift her head to kiss her more intensely.

His mouth seemed to burn her and she felt a wave of pleasure she had never felt before, her body melting and moulding to him of its own free will, her heart racing against his. She realised that for the first time she was kissing him back in a sort of frenzied joy, but no other thought was in her head except a desire to be closer and closer.

Jordan raised his head and they stared at each other, their breathing unsteady. He muttered thickly, his eyes searching her face with the same sort of frenzy she felt inside. 'Dear lord!' he breathed, his voice low and deep in his throat, and then his head bent, capturing her mouth, parting her lips as his hands began to explore her body with an unmistakable necessity.

He unfastened the front of her dress, slipping his hand inside to close over her breast and find it full and swollen. His lips burned a trail across her face and down to her breast, his tongue stroking over the sharp nipple until she felt a wild clamour grow inside that brought a cry of protest and need to her lips. Her fingers laced into his hair and his teeth bit her gently, his low groan making her shiver.

His lips came back to hers, his hand clenching on her breast, and she realised that she was moving beneath him with a vehement need that was stimulating his own primitive reaction to her. Her whole body was shaking and leaping, heat flaring over her. She was going up in flames and she tried to control her mind, stiffening against him, fighting for breath, only realising that she was sobbing his name aloud when she felt his fingers fastening her dress, his hands firmly moving hers which still clung to him.

She was on her feet, his strength steadying her, before she had really come back to her senses and found his eyes on her, deeply assessing.

'Why were you so deeply attached to that Italian?' he asked in a sort of low growl. 'You're utterly unawakened. Nobody has ever touched you. Maybe he gave you a few chaste kisses, but you can take it from me he never intended to go further, and you didn't react to him at all. If you had, he would have gone the whole way, unless he's a cardboard cut-out!'

She just stared at him, unable to speak, her will still utterly subdued to his.

'Grow up, Cassy!' he rasped. 'Start living! It's certain that I'll not help you into this world again, not unless you're prepared to move in here and live with me until this engagement is over. The next time you're on fire in my arms, I'll keep right on going.'

He didn't say a word on the way to her flat, and Cassy was incapable of speech. In any case, she didn't dare to open her mouth. Jordan was like a simmering explosive force beside her, and when he dropped her off she almost fell into her flat, locking the door and staying right there, leaning against the cold, hard wood.

She wanted him! She wanted Jordan so fiercely that she bit her lips together, feeling no pain at all. The pain was all inside, wrapped around with the knowledge that she was more alone than ever.

What would she do? There was time to live out at the office, journeys to his home to see his father. Some inner certainty made her sure that he would never let her leave. His father would want to know why, and so would the people at the office.

Who was to blame? She did not really need to ask that, she already knew. She had forced all this right from the beginning, softening to him when he did not expect it, almost begging to be kissed right here at her own flat simply because he had been kind and thoughtful. She couldn't cope with kindness, she was incapable of reacting properly, normally. She had thought herself cool and businesslike, but Jordan had shown her exactly what she was and he had left an aching need in her that she knew would not go.

CHAPTER EIGHT

AS IT TURNED out, there was no need to face Jordan next day, or for the rest of the week. He rang just as she was leaving for the office, his voice tightly controlled, coldly civilised.

'You'll need to know where I'll be for the next few days,' he informed her. 'Both the editor and deputy editor of the *Gazette* are off with flu. I'm going over there at once and you'd better be clued up before anyone else, under the circumstances.'

'All right. Thank you.' Cassy was at a loss as to how to continue this conversation. Did she mention last night? Would he? She knew that normally their own deputy editor would have been dispatched to stand in at the *Gazette*. It was a paper within the Reece Group and this sort of interchange was not unusual. It was unusual for the editor to go himself, though, especially when the editor was the son of the chairman and major stock holder of the chain. He was going so that he would not have to face her in front of people. Clearly, after last night, they could not go on normally.

'Is there anything that you want me to do?' she asked tremulously, her mind running over the Christmas party and the planning.

'Not a thing,' he said coldly. 'I'll see you when I get back to the office—three or four days, probably.'

He put the phone down and Cassy stood there just looking at it. The whole thing was impossible now. From the first it had been Jordan who had stage-managed this engagement. He had been the one to put all the effort into it, and originally she had hardly co-operated at all. Now he would no longer be able to even act the part at his parents' home. In the office it would be one long misery for both of them.

At least she was able to play her part when she got to work.

'Jordan's away for a few days,' she said at once, before anyone could ask where he was and be told by Barry Stock, the deputy editor. They all went into the morning conference knowing as much as Cassy knew herself, and it all seemed to be normal; naturally she would know as soon as Barry, or even before. As Jordan was not there to praise this bit of foresight, she didn't get a lot of satisfaction from it and she knew that the days would drag without him.

He called her on Friday evening, and he was less terse than he had been before.

'Tomorrow I'm going down to see Dad,' he said briskly, no inflection in his voice that would give her a clue to his thoughts. 'Do you intend to come with me?'

'Of course!' Recognising her tendency to battle, she stifled the anger that welled up inside. 'Isn't that what it's all about? In any case, you know I want to see your father.'

'Very well,' he agreed quietly. 'I'll collect you at about one o'clock. There's no reason to be off earlier. Saturday traffic is fairly sparse on the motorway at this time of the year, and my mother is staying at a hotel for the time being.'

'Why?' Cassy felt left out that he had not told her this before, and she had to remind herself that this was Jordan's home, these were his parents and nothing to do with her at all.

'It's a long way to travel to the hospital and she's none too keen on driving. The house is a little isolated too, not a good place for her to stay alone. I moved her last weekend.'

'I—I see.' She was beginning to be hurt by the cold voice, and she couldn't think of a thing to say anyway.

'Anything else?' Jordan asked tightly. He was back where he had always been, and she remembered her thoughts of him before all this had happened. She had not been mistaken, after all; he was cold, hard and impatient.

'Not a thing!' she snapped. 'I'll be ready for one tomorrow.'

This time *she* put the phone down, knowing that if this conversation continued she would give him a piece of her mind. How she could have been wildly inflamed in his arms she did not know. He was flying his old colours now with a vengeance, his true colours! She put her coat on and went out to the shops. Just because Jordan Reece infuriated her, there was no reason to be anything other than normal with his parents. She liked them and she took pleasure in searching for a little gift for each of them; she stayed out late doing it. When he grimly collected her next day she had the gifts wrapped and in her suitcase.

His eyes flared coldly over her as she came out—the very look he used to give her—and she flushed with anger.

'Am I suitably dressed?' she snapped, unable to keep quiet after such a long, cool inspection. 'If I offend, I'm quite prepared to go back and change!'

'You do not offend,' he assured her calmly. 'You're always beautifully dressed.'

'Then why the long look of disapproval?' she demanded angrily.

'I wasn't disapproving,' he said in an even voice. 'I was considering whether you're going to be warm enough in that short skirt, or I was admiring your legs. Take your pick!'

It was more than enough to silence her and he started off without more ado, turning out of the town and heading for the nearest motorway entrance along cold, almost deserted roads.

The weather had stabilised over the week, and here there were just lingering patches of snow, the hillsides edged with white, the fields dappled with the icy remains. They stopped for a quick and silent afternoon tea and then they were moving again, travelling quickly south, Jordan silent and impassive, his long, perfect hands on the wheel, his eyes on the road ahead, and Cassy sank lower into her seat, trying not to give in to her usual urge to look at him.

She began to pick up vibes however as they progressed and finally turned on to normal roads to head across country. The snow had not gone here. In some places it was icily banked beside the road, and she saw Jordan's eyes assessing the situation. If more snow fell, this area was going to be quite bad. They would have to hope that the forecast was right and that the snow had finished until after the Christmas holiday.

'Where are we going to stay?' Cassy wanted to know as they arrived at last in town.

'I thought it would be a good idea to stay in the same hotel as Mother,' he said stiffly. 'It would be the most natural thing to do, unless you have any great objection?'

'None at all,' Cassy said frostily, adding with a certain amount of spite, 'I'll pay for myself!'

'I got you into a situation that you couldn't get out of without a fight,' he admitted. 'I'm a bit too strong to fight, so naturally you used your very sharp tongue. I should have expected nothing less, knowing you as I do.' He shrugged and smiled tightly. 'Unfortunately, it was a little too sharp. It hurt!'

'I hurt *you*?' Cassy asked in utter bewilderment, her brown eyes large and shocked.

'My ego, Cassy,' he confessed with a wry look. 'No man likes to think that when he's kissing a woman she's busy calculating the reason for it. She's supposed to be swept off her feet!'

'It was because I was—was off my feet that . . .' Cassy muttered, turning away, not knowing what to say at all. He was taking the blame for her, ignoring how she had persistently thrown herself at him. She was too filled with confusion to even begin to sort herself out.

'That was my fault, too,' he said with a terse laugh at her remark. 'I just went for you and accused you of wanting to be best all the time. If I'd kept quiet, you wouldn't have fallen.'

'It doesn't matter,' Cassy said quietly. 'We can't expect to behave like normal people, can we? We just basically dislike each other, we have from the first. It's unfortunate that it had to be me, that's all.'

'True,' he murmured sardonically. 'But as it has to be you, then we'll have to make the best of it. Let's go and join my mother.'

She darted back as they went out and opened her uitcase, getting out the beautifully wrapped gift.

'I—I brought a little gift for your mother and another or your father,' she said as he looked at her in surprise. hope you don't mind,' she added as he stared at her ith narrowed eyes.

'Don't be tiresome, Cassy,' Jordan murmured q 'Things will obviously be very difficult, without display of childish spite. I'm relying on your affectio for my father to see us through this, but try to remember that I would make a very bad and determined enemy!'

It was not so much the words he used as the quiet tone that made him sound menacing, and it also made her feel ashamed of her burst of spite—childish spite. Cassy sat in silence and he ignored her completely.

He booked them in and took her along to her room, and then he disappeared to find his mother and Cassy realised that this was the flavour of things to come. If she wanted to be one of the family then she would have to push her way forward. Unfortunately, she wasn't capable of that sort of thing. She was good at her job, quite well able to be pushy there, but in family matters she had always taken a back seat, been on the very edge of things, and she could not enthuse and gush over people, she feared rejection too much for that.

She had unpacked all the small necessities and was sitting rather disconsolately on the edge of the bed w Jordan came back, tapping on the door and comin at her rather empty-voiced invitation.

'We're in the downstairs coffee lounge,' he abruptly. 'If you could summon up a smile of so think you should join us.'

She didn't say anything. She simply picked up h and walked to the door, but he stopped her as she to walk past.

'Cassy,' he said quietly, 'I'm sorry about th night.'

It was so unexpected that she just stood quite stared up at him, not knowing how to reply t all.

'If you want to, then of course I don't mind,' hc said slowly. 'If you feel you have to...'

'Why should I?' Cassy said quickly, looking away from his intent stare. 'I like them, oddly enough!'

'Oddly enough, they like you too,' he said softly, taking her shoulders as she tried to pass. 'Oddly enough, so do I.' He looked down at her as she stood utterly stiff and unyielding. 'It's just unfortunate that you rub me up the wrong way, but I expect that's due to your instant antagonism to me. All things considered, you've done well so far. Let's bury the hatchet and begin again.'

Not when she was feeling like this! Not when his hands on her shoulders were burning her skin even through her jacket. One mistake, one soft glance from him and she would be right back to the other night, mindless and moaning.

'We don't need to,' she got out rapidly, pulling away fast. 'We've nearly reached the end of this.'

'The end?' he said in astonishment. 'What about Christmas? What about the time after until Dad is well enough to take the blow? We've only just begun!'

'I—I can't...' she said desperately as he pulled her back to look at him. 'I can't go through all that again. We don't have to pretend so hard now, they believe it all. I just can't go on—being...'

'Being close to me!' he finished for her angrily. 'We're in this too deep for any backsliding now,' he rasped. 'Whatever your personal revulsions are, you'll have to fight them. Start now!'

Before she could move he caught her close, his lips hard on hers, anger making him almost cruel, and he was too big, too strong to fight against. She tried to stiffen as heat grew from her toes and spread fiercely through her but he felt her inner fighting and merely tightened her to him, forcing her lips apart and making her accept his kiss totally.

When his lips softened she was already lost, her hands lifeless against him as anger and fear drained away and a sweet lethargy took its place. He raised his head and looked down at her intently, and her face flushed as she met his clear silver gaze.

'You—you said that you would never...' she began tremulously.

'In the anger of the moment I forget that with you it's essential!' he muttered. 'Left to yourself, you'd probably interview my parents with a shorthand notebook in your hand.' He strode from the room and she had no choice but to follow, but he wasn't leaving her in any case; he locked her door and handed her the key, and as she would have walked off huffily he took her arm and slowed her pace to his.

'You're on stage, Cassy,' he warned quietly as they came to the door of the coffee lounge, 'from this moment until we're on our way back!'

She knew it, and when he took her hand she made no effort to get free, even though it seemed to send shocks all the way up her arm.

Cassy was greeted so warmly that she felt tearfully bewildered. Dorothy Reece had made her mind up that her future daughter-in-law was exactly what she wanted, and when they visited Jordan's father his joy and pride were almost tangible. He had his family around him, a family that was going to grow. He looked so much better already, and Cassy knew that she would find it hard to ever tell this kindly man that his dreams were not to be realised.

Jordan too was warm and gentle, his acting ability such that Cassy felt that Lavinia would have been very impressed. Where would they get the necessary acting ability to convince a loving couple that it was all a mistake and not a great lie? As she sat beside Jordan on the return journey late next afternoon she felt that she could not go on with this for much longer. She was almost in tears with guilt and misery, and it kept her grimly silent.

Snow began to fall long before they reached the motorway, and almost immediately visibility became difficult. The flakes were fat and heavy, swirling blindingly towards them driven by a rising wind, and as they turned on to the motorway they found the hazard warning lights were already on, advising lower and lower speeds as they progressed.

'We can't carry on in this!' Jordan muttered, breaking a long silence. 'Pretty soon we're going to be merely crawling along. I don't fancy being in a great tailback of traffic here, there's always some fool who knows better. We'll get off at the next exit.'

'Won't it be worse across country?' Cassy asked a trifle anxiously. She had put on thick woollen tights and high boots, and she was glad of it. If they were stranded, then at least she would be warm; she even had her fur hat.

'Maybe,' Jordan said grimly. 'At least we'll be under our own steam, masters of our own fate.' He began to signal as the exit signs came up, and soon they were on normal roads, although the conditions were no better. 'If it's too bad, at least we can stop at a hotel for the night somewhere,' he said evenly. 'We're not too far from the nearest town.'

Cassy had no idea where they were, the driving snow seemed to have closed them into an unreal world, and although they were warm and comfortable in the car she was as aware as Jordan that should they be forced to stop it would not be long before they were really cold. The snow was thick already here, too. They had not seen this part of the country coming down, but it was obvious now that in this low-lying part the snow had remained. Now more was piling on top of it.

'I think we should stop,' Jordan said after a few miles. 'There's no point in risking being stranded in the middle of nowhere. The next place we see, OK?' Cassy could only agree; in fact, she had no idea how he was able to see now.

It was Cassy, though, who spotted the lights of a village just off the main road, and Jordan drove towards it through deeper and deeper snow. He was grimly silent and Cassy knew that, like her, he was wondering if there was such a thing as an inn or if they would be forced to continue. A few miles more and they would have no choice but to stop anyway, so it was worth the risk of turning off here.

They crawled through the village, Cassy straining her eyes to find some place to stay and greatly relieved when a sign announced that there was after all an inn, the Spotted Calf.

'Thank heavens for that!' Jordan muttered, blinking his eyes after the strain of driving. 'Let's get straight in and see what they can come up with.'

They were not the only ones there. Jordan could only just get the car off the road, and Cassy hoped that the other cars held locals and not people who had followed their own decision and made for a refuge for the night.

It was warm and noisy inside, and Cassy stuck tightly by Jordan as he pushed his way to the bar.

'I hope you have overnight accommodation,' he told the rosy-cheeked woman who smiled pleasantly at them.

'Only just, sir!' She laughed. 'We've been overwhelmed by visitors for the last hour. I expect you've done the same as the rest, got off the motorway for the night?'

'That's right,' Jordan said. 'Can you let us have...'

'Just a minute, sir, I'll get my husband. He's been doing the rooms for these people. I'd hate to tell you we'd got somewhere left and then have him say we hadn't!'

They had, and Cassy sighed with relief as they were led upstairs.

'You can get your things later,' the landlord said comfortably. 'I'll just show you and give you the key, and then you can manage by yourselves—we're a bit busy right now. You can have some supper later, if you like.'

'Thanks, we will,' Jordan assured him. 'Cassy?' he added with a quick look at her, and she nodded, even managing a swift smile. It was a minor miracle to have found somewhere first go.

'Here we are!' The landlord opened a heavy, oaken door and ushered them in. 'The last room in the place! You're the luckiest couple. Another half-hour and this would have been gone for sure, we're the last place for miles!'

'You've only the one room?' Jordan asked with a great restraint in his voice that Cassy knew covered considerable impatience. 'We wanted two, actually.'

'I'm sorry, sir. This is it. We haven't another nook or cranny, and as I said, we're the last place for miles. I expect you'll be able to manage here,' he added, glancing at Cassy, his eyes moving to her ring, 'leastways, nobody's going to ask any questions on a night like this!'

He left them to it, his chuckle apparently annoying Jordan and certainly embarrassing Cassy. Her eyes seemed to be glued to the big double bed, and she stood stiffly in the doorway with no intention of moving.

'What are we going to do?' she asked tightly when Jordan simply began to explore the room calmly.

'Make the best of it. Manage, as the man said. We have little or no alternative. You were here and heard everything. This is the only accommodation for miles. We're damned lucky to get it!'

'I don't feel so damned lucky at the moment!' Cassy assured him heatedly, her face flushed with embarrassment. 'That object that almost fills this room is a double bed.'

'Thank your stars it's not a single bed,' Jordan bit out. 'For heaven's sake, Cassy, you know the circumstances as well as I do; even your inbuilt dislike and distrust of me can't lead you to believe that I planned this!'

'Well, we'll—we'll have to come up with some arrangement,' Cassy muttered.

'I sleep on the bar and you occupy the bed?' Jordan asked sardonically. 'No, thank you, Miss Preston! That object is quite big enough for two. We'll make a barrier of pillows right down the middle if you feel it necessary, or we can sit up all night and stare at the bed, first to fall asleep loses. In case you haven't noticed,' he added irascibly, 'there's no central heating in here. You've just recovered from flu and I'm not suicidal! We'll go and get some supper, and then we'll arrange two separate armed camps and get some sleep. With a bit of luck, we'll be on our way tomorrow. Even here at the back of beyond I imagine they have snow ploughs!'

She couldn't fault his logic and there seemed to be nothing more to say. Even now, with her coat on, the cold was beginning to bite a little and she knew perfectly well that they had been miraculously lucky to find this place. She went down to supper anxious but convinced that Jordan was right, as usual.

It was a different matter when it was time to actually contemplate the night's arrangements, though. If they had been friends, if they had been used to laughing together, it wouldn't have mattered so much. Cassy wished herself back to the warm and companionable time of her flu when she had been just recovering and been so reliant on Jordan. If things had still been like that she wouldn't have minded. She had been able to laugh with him then, he had been almost gentle.

Things were not by any means the same now, though, and she had not liked the wry smile that the landlady had given her; no doubt the woman thought that this little stop-over would strengthen their attachment to each other. She had seen the woman's admiring eyes on her engagement ring. If only she knew!

'You can go along to the bathroom first,' Jordan said coolly as they came back upstairs after supper and he had brought their cases from the car. 'You can then get ready for bed here while I go. I'll change in the bathroom.'

Cassy more or less fled, feeling quite stupid that she was making so much of this, and when she got back she changed more quickly then she had ever done in her life. When Jordan came back she was standing in her nightie and dressing-gown and her eyes moved with shocked appraisal over him as he came into the room in a black towelling robe.

'Sorry to alarm you, but I don't carry pyjamas around with me,' he said irritably. 'I expect central heating. Don't panic, I have every intention of sleeping in my robe!'

'What—which...' Cassy began helplessly, and he glanced at her wryly.

'Oh, lady's choice, naturally,' he said quietly. 'Choose your side of the bed. It makes little difference, after all; both sides join in the middle.'

It embarrassed her into rushing round to the farthest side, taking off her dressing-gown and flinging herself into bed and under the sheets. It was only when she was in there that she remembered they had not made a barrier of pillows, and as there were few enough pillows, anyway, she gave up the idea. She didn't fancy seeing the landlady's face if they demanded more!

The bed sank a little as Jordan switched off the light and came to bed immediately.

'You'd be well advised to keep your dressing-gown on,' he remarked quietly.

'I'm perfectly well covered up!' Cassy snapped without thought.

'I wasn't thinking of your modesty,' Jordan rasped. 'I've just about done everything for you but change your nightie when you were ill! I was thinking about the cold.'

'I'm quite warm,' Cassy lied. 'We're not on Everest!'

'Tell me that in the middle of the night when you're shivering,' Jordan taunted. 'In any case, if we were on a cold mountain, we'd probably be both in one sleeping-bag. The need to survive makes strange bedfellows.'

Cassy didn't answer. She was too busy trying to get warm. There was no way she was going to get out of bed again and admit that she should have kept her dressing-gown on. She lay stiffly at her edge of the bed and tucked her feet up into her nightie, folded her hands under her arms and tried to sleep.

It was light in the room when she awoke, and instinctively she knew that it was partly the brightness of snow.

She was blissfully warm and comfortable, and that was because she was snuggled tightly up to Jordan, his arm around her. Her heart almost stopped when she realised that in the night she had moved, searching like a small animal for warmth.

She began to move stealthily away, but even that slight movement disturbed him and he sighed, turning towards her, his other arm encircling her waist, trapping her securely. Apart from wrenching herself away and awakening him, seeing the disdain on his face then, there was nothing she could do. She would have to lie still until he woke up, and then pretend she was asleep until he moved.

She tried to relax and his breathing seemed to deepen, but his arm stayed firmly in place, his hand across the flat of her stomach and she lay quietly, watching him. Asleep, he was utterly without harshness. His dark lashes brushed his cheeks, his hair was ruffled across his forehead, those firm lips warmly relaxed, almost sensuous.

A feeling of tenderness flooded through Cassy, a feeling she had never felt before, and a smile edged her lips as she carefully put out her hand and touched his face. She wanted to love him, to hold him tightly, to kiss that cool, handsome face without him knowing. Her fingers stroked his cheek, lingering like the soft touch of silk, and she knew all at once why she had wanted him so wildly, why she had moved to him when he had been at her flat. Against all odds, she loved him. She loved him deeply and completely.

It was not the rather childish feeling she had mistaken for love with Luigi; that had been because, erroneously, she had felt that someone cared about her. This time, she was the one caring. Jordan had been kind for a little while and she had let him into her heart, even though he had no wish to be there. It was astonishing. It was a feeling that seemed to fill every part of her. She trailed her fingers delicately over his lips, utterly lost in her own discovery, her eyes wide and wondering as she gazed at him.

'Don't you know that it's very dangerous to do that to a man first thing in the morning?'

Jordan's voice, deep and quiet, startled her into snatching her hand away, and she tried to dive to her own side of the bed. He merely tightened his arms around her, his hand clasping her waist.

'I—in the night I—I must have moved...' she began nervously, fighting to control panic.

'I know,' he murmured mockingly. 'I awoke to find myself in the midst of a territorial battle, and as I was losing, I took restraining measures.' He tightened his arm around her. 'Afterwards, you subsided. I told you that you wouldn't like it on Everest.'

'Shouldn't—shouldn't we get up now?' Cassy stammered anxiously, but he merely continued to gaze at her with half-closed eyes, a smile playing around the edge of his mouth.

'It's only seven. I doubt if anyone is about yet. When I get up, I like breakfast at once. Besides, it's cold.'

His eyes began to move over her, amused as he glanced at the frilly neck of her nightie.

'I remember thinking when you were ill what a strange person you were,' he murmured. 'You walk around in short skirts, lovely long legs clear for all to see, and then at night, when there's nobody there to see at all, you wear a long-sleeved, demure nightie that wouldn't disgrace Grandma. I thought at one time that it was because you wanted to be looked at during the day, but I knew you a little too well by then and changed my mind instantly.'

His fingers trailed down the small, neat buttons and then moved to cup her breast softly and gently, and she gasped, looking at him with bewildered eyes.

'I want to look at you now, Cassy,' he said quietly as she stared, hypnotised into the silvery eyes.

'Jordan!' Her voice was shaking and he heard it, his hand moving to capture hers.

'Let's go right back to the beginning,' he urged softly. 'I woke up and you were touching me. Touch me again, Cassy!'

He put her hand to his face and she didn't move it away; her eyes were entranced as they followed the movement of her fingers across the silken rasp of his skin. As she touched his lips, he took her hand gently, kissing each fingertip; she'd not known how much rapture could come from so small an act. As her eyes closed, he lifted her towards him, his hand cradling her head, his other moulding her breast gently until she sought blindly for his lips and his mouth opened over hers.

Sweet tenderness flooded through her as he kissed and stroked her, every part of her coming to warm life and eagerness, unafraid as she felt his fingers slipping the buttons of her nightie, a gasp of pleasure murmured against his mouth as his hand closed over the warmth of her breast.

'Warm, beautiful Cassy,' he whispered against her lips, and it brought her partly back to sanity, to memory of the warmly lit room, the soft lights and the Christmas tree. Was he kissing her because she had moved close, because he thought she needed it?

'No, Cassy,' he said quietly, his eyes no longer sleepy but vibrant on her face as he moved his hand to caress her hot cheeks. 'Nothing therapeutic. This is sheer necessity!'

His eyes slid over the demure nightie which was softly sprigged with flowers, and he smiled.

'Even this didn't keep you warm, did it? I kept you warm.' He raised his eyes to hers, holding her gaze. 'Let me take it off,' he said softly.

She knew that she was spellbound, locked in some timeless place with Jordan. At the back of her mind every instinct, every tiny bit of knowledge that life had painfully drilled into her warned her that this was not real, that he would leave her readily enough when this time was over. But she was enchanted by his gentleness, utterly lost in her newly discovered love, and when his hand slid over her slender hip, moving upwards and bringing the nightie with it, she turned into his arms, her hands languorous against his chest, moving almost dreamily to slide beneath his thick robe and caress his shoulders.

'Cassy!' With one swift movement he pulled the garment over her head and tossed it aside before shrugging out of his robe to urge her hands back to their bewildered caressing of his skin.

His hand, powerful and strong, moved with restless energy from her shoulder to her hip, turning her closer towards him, and then he cupped her face impatiently, his eyes burning silver as he looked down at her.

'That's the first time in my whole life that I've ever wanted to actually tear the clothes off a woman,' he muttered thickly. 'Your first lover should be gentle, Cassy. But I want you too damned much!'

His mouth drove down on hers and all the languorous warmth left her, to be replaced by fiery strength. Her arms wound around his neck and she kissed him back wildly until they were both gasping for breath.

For a second, he pushed her away to trace her body with restless fingers, his eyes hotly on her breast that even then rose towards him, sharp and pinkly tipped, aching as his fingers traced a circle of fire around it. His kisses were burning, branding her with heat as they moved over her face and neck, his teeth nipping at her skin until her whole body trembled.

But she was again the being he had known once before, wild and burning in his arms, her reaction forcing the same gasp from his throat.

'You're incredible!' he muttered fiercely. 'You turn into fire the moment I touch you.'

He kissed her hungrily until she was moving against him with mindless pleasure, small pleading sounds forced from her throat, and Jordan seemed to have lost all control of his actions. He moved over her, his powerful body subduing her, stilling her frantic movements. For one second, his eyes blazed into hers, probing and questioning, and she arched against him as his hands slid to her thighs.

Her vision blurred, became a swirl of shimmering stars that were the wild echoes of her heartbeat and the glittering silver of Jordan's eyes.

'Jordan . . .' Her voice was far away, faint, on the very edge of consciousness, the pleading shaken and soft and his lips closed over hers with a shock of tenderness as he possessed her.

She leapt in his arms, her eyes opening wide, and his hand stroked over her face, his eyes holding hers before he closed her lips with hunger and took her out of the world into timeless, velvet night.

Later he held her against him as she lay with her face buried into his shoulder, and dimly she realised that she was sobbing his name, her fingers still digging into his skin. She was another person, afraid to move out of his arms and come back to life in the silent room. For a long time she had left it, left the world, and the experience had shaken her more than she could imagine.

She clutched at him as he moved and he took her with him, his hand stroking back her hair as he watched her face.

'Nobody has ever done that before with me,' he said in a strange voice. 'For one or two seconds, you weren't there at all. How do you feel?'

Totally reborn, another person, her whole being changed. The thoughts whirled through her head as she looked back into his eyes. Now, though, she remembered some of the words. 'Your first lover should be gentle.' It was passion to Jordan, nothing more. It was only to be expected that a man like Jordan would have deep, passionate feelings hidden inside, and once again she had forced the pace, she had moved to him, touched him.

'I'm all right,' she managed breathlessly. 'A little stunned, perhaps...'

It was as bright a voice as she could manage. She sought quickly in her mind to come up with what a blithe modern person would say at a time like this.

'Cassy!' His voice was suddenly edged with anger, his hand tightening on her face.

'I'm fine, really,' she said with a brittle smile. 'Don't you think we should get up and view the weather?'

For a moment he simply looked at her, his gaze narrowed and probing, but all he got was an embarrassed glance and an impatient movement, and he moved too, shrugging into his robe and belting it around him.

'You're a lost cause, Cassy,' he bit out, his voice tight and strained. 'You've given me the most astonishing and beautiful experience of my life, and you're instantly back to normal, the mundane matters of the weather and the necessity to get moving back at the top of your mind.'

She was stunned at the sound of his voice, the bitterness, the words. The most beautiful experience of his life. Did he mean that? Even if he did, what was the future? A temporary engagement, a mutual secret and, finally, Jordan back to the life he really wanted.

'Jordan——' she murmured, bewildered at the look on his face.

'Forget it!' he said harshly. 'I'll get dressed and then go down to see what's happening while you get dressed. Stay here for the time being.'

He walked out, collecting his clothes and slamming the door, utterly uncaring if he raised the whole of the inn with noise, and Cassy's eyes filled with tears. She had been better, safer, without love. Of all the hurts of her life, nothing had hurt like this.

CHAPTER NINE

THE SNOW ploughs had been out during the night and early morning, and after a silent breakfast they continued their journey northwards. Jordan was tight-lipped and cool as she had never seen him before, and Cassy felt utterly lost. Dimly she realised that under normal circumstances she would have felt cheap. He had made love to her fiercely and now he even refused to speak to her at all. It was true that she had made the first move but, even so, Jordan had encouraged her, had never drawn back, and she asked herself if she really knew him at all. It had always been Jordan who drew back. How would he be now if she had stayed dreamily in his arms? Had she really driven him to anger and disgust, or was this his excuse to disclaim any responsibility for what had happened?

There had never been the slightest intention on either part to prolong this arrangement, and now things had changed. They could not be allowed to change, but she could not shake off the feeling that her world was now a different place. She had not one regret. She had been transformed, but she could not expect Jordan to feel like that. It wasn't just that it was the first time for her, either. Something deep and lasting had happened that had left her feeling strange and weak but warmer inside than she had felt in the whole of her life.

She glanced secretly at Jordan's tense face, her eyes wondering, her lips parted. I belong to him! The words were brilliant in her mind, and she knew that they would be there for always. If anyone else ever tried to claim her, she would be shocked beyond belief; it would be outrageous! She belonged to Jordan.

He glanced across as if he felt her startled appraisal, and for one telling second their eyes met, Cassy unable to look away. He turned his attention back to the road, but his lips were tighter than ever and she could feel anger radiating from him. She had become a responsibility that he did not want, his whole attitude told her that. It didn't matter. She had no intention whatever of becoming a responsibility. She could live for the rest of her life on the love that had happened so swiftly and fiercely.

As he stopped at her flat she got straight out, beginning as she meant to go on, but Jordan was out at the same time, his hand on her suitcase with no intention of letting it go. She shrugged and opened the door of her flat, turning to take the case from him, but he came in, closing the door and facing her squarely.

'I intend to go straight into the office,' he said firmly. 'You do not.'

'How do you know what I intend to do?' Cassy asked sharply, her cool response hiding shaken emotions as she looked up at him. She walked into her sitting-room, but he followed determinedly.

'Before we face each other at work, with so many interested eyes on us, I want to talk to you. We'll talk tonight,' he insisted.

'As we're both several hours late already,' Cassy pointed out, 'I can't see the need to rush into work. If we have anything to talk about, then let's get it over with at once. To begin with, you can now surely see the need for one of us to move? Things are going to be more difficult than ever now. I'll point out what I said before.

I must be the one to move, and I must start that move as soon as possible.'

'I cannot and will not agree,' Jordan said angrily. 'The reasons are still the same, but now, after this morning, there's one big difference. I want this engagement to be real. I want to marry you and take care of you!'

Cassy stood perfectly still and looked at him in utter bewilderment. Everything inside her turned over with joy for one wonderful second only. Surely she had expected this, after all, coming as it did from Jordan. He had given up what he wanted to do because his father was ill and had asked him, now he intended to give his own life up permanently because of one moment of passion, a passion that had now clearly died. She sought frantically for her old attitude to cloak her.

'Do I look like the sort of person who needs taking care of?' she asked coldly, a quizzical smile on her face. 'I think you've forgotten who I am, Jordan. I have a career of my own and I intend to go right on with it. I'm not the little wife type!'

'Have I asked you to give up anything?' he questioned angrily.

'Only my freedom,' Cassy retorted sharply, and for a long time he just stood and looked at her before turning abruptly and leaving the flat. She walked to the window and watched him drive away, but even then no tears fell. There were no tears anywhere near. The warm, magical feeling refused to go. She belonged to the grim-faced man who drove off at such an alarming speed, but he would never know, must never know quite how she felt. It was just something that had happened. There was no need for Jordan to suffer because of it, no need for him to tie himself down for life. After all, it had not happened to him, it had happened to her. She didn't go to work, though. She had enough sense to know that she was not geared up to tackle anyone like Claud Ackland. She had to sleep on it first.

When she did go, she walked into an entirely new state of affairs. Jordan ignored her and it was noticed.

'What's up, Cass?' Guy asked quietly after a couple of days when it was so obvious that even Claud made no comment.

'We had a spat,' Cassy said lightly. It was no use whatever pretending otherwise, and to confess to a small thing seemed wise. It might keep the wolves at bay for a while.

'Is it all off, then?' Guy asked gloomily. The engagement had made them all feel just a little more secure with Jordan's power. Cassy was one of their own and they never doubted that she would fight for them if the need arose.

'Of course not!' Cassy said quickly. 'People quarrel, you know. How could it be off?' How, indeed, with Jordan's mother ringing her about Christmas, his father getting stronger by the day and expecting them both to be there on the festive days?

She went into Jordan's office when she had a minute, and shut the door firmly.

'You once told me that you were being the horse and the cart,' she said at once, wading in in her old manner. 'Now I'm the complete team by myself. People are noticing. Do you want to do anything about it?'

'What, for example?' Jordan asked tersely, barely glancing at her, his eyes straight back to the work he was doing.

'Well, what about this Christmas party, for a start?' Cassy asked.

'The hell with a Christmas party!' he snapped, his eyes flashing like frosty light. 'I'm taking the tree down tonight.'

'That's bad luck!' Cassy exclaimed in outrage.

'No,' he said quietly. 'The bad luck was putting it up in the first place.' He went right back to what he was doing and Cassy came to his desk, her temper flaring.

'So far,' she snapped, 'you've been the one to ask if I wanted this to be all over. Now I'm asking you. Your mother phoned last night to discuss Christmas. You said she wasn't to be hurt and I've no intention of hurting either of them. Have you?'

'You know damned well I haven't,' he rasped, standing and towering over her.

'Then shall we get on with things?' Cassy asked sharply. 'Having been given no real idea of what you wanted to do with a Christmas gathering, I've come up with a few arrangements for you to look at. If you can manage to make your mind up today, then I'll get on with it!'

'Get on with what?' he asked angrily. 'All I ever asked you to do was help me to plan it.'

'I've done my share of that,' Cassy told him firmly. 'See what you want and I'll get on with the organisation.'

'Why?' he asked quietly, coming round the desk to her. 'What's got into you?'

'I'm just trying to move things along,' Cassy said briskly, anxious about him being close but determined to hold her ground. 'You're sitting snugly in here, I'm the one with questions to answer. A party at your house would shut everyone up, if we can manage to be civil towards each other!'

'All right,' he agreed slowly. 'I'll look at any plans and let you know as soon as possible.'

'Like before we leave tonight,' Cassy said triumphantly, handing him a notebook. 'They're all in here.'

He glanced at the book she had almost slammed into his hand, and some of the tightness left his face as a smile flickered around the edge of his mouth.

'And what about Christmas at home?' he asked quietly, his eyes intently on her face.

'We have no alternative but to go,' Cassy informed him as she turned to the door, her trembling hands in her pockets. 'The snow gives us an excuse to stay away until then, but obviously your mother is going to ring me again and I'm not telling her that we can't go.'

'Unless the weather stops us,' he remarked casually, but the tone of his voice brought a quick flush to her face. It would have been better not to mention the snow, not to remind him. She went out quickly, knowing what she had known for a couple of days. The glow was beginning to fade and a deep ache was taking its place.

By the end of January Cassy had good reason to remember Christmas. The party at Jordan's house had been a raging success. He had announced it out of the blue, only Cassy knowing beforehand, and he had used the announcement to good measure, inviting them all quite informally and beginning with the words, 'Cassy and I would be very pleased if you would all come for a small party before Christmas.' He had come to stand with his arm around her, and it seemed to Cassy that the whole place breathed a sigh of relief.

Not much acting had been needed after that, but Cassy's evening had been clouded with one big worry. Now, over a month later, the worry had become a certainty: she was pregnant. Deep down, she had known for far longer. Perhaps her feeling of being transformed had been some miraculous warning of this, and Christmas with Jordan's parents had been a wonderful thing for her.

There had been everything that she had ever imagined Christmas to be: the log fires, the holly and mistletoe, the shining, glittering tree with presents around it, the smell of good things cooking and people dropping in at all times to greet them all.

Harold Reece was home, looking well though a trifle shaken, but it had not stopped him from enjoying Christmas with great relish. Cassy had eagerly helped with the cooking, delighting in Dorothy Reece's wry humour and odd little ways. She almost forgot that this was not real.

On Christmas Day, just before dinner, she had been alone in the kitchen finishing a sauce when Jordan strolled in, his face still warm and smiling from an encounter with his father, and the smile still remained as he took her arm and led her to the middle of the room.

'What are you doing?' Cassy asked fretfully. 'The sauce will be ruined!' He just pointed to the ceiling and the bunch of mistletoe hanging there.

'I'm working my way into the Christmas spirit,' he said drily, taking her flushed face in his hands and kissing her before she could even move.

A second later and she couldn't move. He never had to force her to this, never had to plead. She moved into his arms as he reached for her, and he deepened the kiss until she was shaking, the sauce and its fate forgotten.

'You can't keep away from me,' he murmured against her lips, 'so why pretend otherwise? Marry me, Cassy!'

'There's more to marriage than kissing,' Cassy managed breathlessly, trying to pull away and failing completely. 'I've no intention of marrying. I've seen a marriage, thank you!'

'My parents' marriage isn't like that,' Jordan said impatiently, his eyes burning into hers. 'Why should ours be?'

'Oh, please, Jordan!' she said scathingly. 'Your mother and father love each other. My mother and father at least thought they did. We *know* that we don't.'

'Damn you, Cassy!' he grated, his voice thick and low. 'I want you and you want me.'

'I don't,' Cassy lied quickly. 'Once was more than enough, and even if I did . . .' She didn't get the chance to say any more, his lips ground into hers, his strength being used deliberately to subdue and silence her, frustration and anger in every taut muscle of his body. There was nothing but violence in him and Cassy went limp, tears coming to her eyes for the first time since he had made love to her.

He lifted his head to look at her and she tore away, running from the kitchen and up to her room. He didn't follow and she pulled herself out of the sudden misery. How could he be like that when she was doing all this for him? She knew perfectly well what it was. His father would have been asking about the wedding date, probably his mother too. Cassy knew they had been expecting a date to be set this Christmas, and Jordan had been angry, guilty. Even then she had been sure deep down that she was pregnant, and she knew without doubt that she must find another job, far away from Jordan before he found out.

By the end of January it was all too real, and there was not one job on the horizon. The morning conferences were becoming a greater nightmare each day. Her eyes refused to look away from Jordan, darting anxiously aside as he looked up at her, and the strain was intolerable.

'Phew! That was sticky,' Guy confided, after they came out. 'It seems to me that he's actually taking our department apart deliberately. Can't you speak to him, Cass?'

'I'll try,' Cassy promised. She felt guilty that today she had dragged Guy in there with her. It was true, Jordan was putting the pressure on hatefully, and this morning she hadn't been able to face him without reinforcements.

She walked in front of Guy back to her desk, glad that he couldn't see the utter misery on her face, and without warning the room began to spin, sound faded. She made a desperate grab for a chair but she was too late, her hands refused to function and she fell at Guy's feet in a faint.

She came round quickly, but not before Guy had crouched down to cradle her head and not before someone had rushed in to get Jordan.

'What is it?' Jordan's face was tight as he knelt beside her, taking over impatiently from Guy, who only gave in reluctantly.

'It's stress,' Guy muttered in annoyance. 'She's had about just as much as she can take! Cass isn't like this. People like Cass just don't faint!'

'Clearly they do!' Jordan bit out. Cassy began to struggle to her feet, but he stood and scooped her up as if she was no weight at all, and somehow it made things worse. His personality was powerful enough, this unthinking, effortless display of physical strength seemed to infuriate Guy.

'Perhaps if you didn't drive her so hard, it wouldn't be necessary to pick her up!' Guy snapped, and Jordan turned completely round to look at him, his eyes icy.

'Shut up, Guy,' he said in a deceptively soft voice. 'Don't make the fatal mistake of stepping between Cassy and me. I know perfectly well what's wrong with her.'

Cassy shut her eyes tightly to close out the sight of Guy's face; she didn't want to see the dawning understanding or the shock. Of all the things Jordan could have said, he had to say that! Not a soul knew that she was pregnant, and they would never know. If a job did not materialise before the end of next month, she would simply leave and move away, maybe get help from her father to set herself up somewhere else far away.

'Please put me down, I can walk perfectly well,' she said quietly as they moved away from intently listening ears.

'Very well.' He set her on her feet but kept a tight grip on her arm. 'I'm taking you home.' He didn't sound as if he would welcome any argument, and Cassy didn't try.

'All right,' she said quietly, and she collected her coat as Jordan moved to get his. Right now she just wanted to get away, all by herself.

He came into her flat and just stood looking at her, following her as she made for the kitchen to get a cup of tea.

'I'll do that,' he said quietly, calmly taking things from her hands.

'I'm not helpless!' Cassy said sharply, her only intention to get him out of here, even to anger him if that would do it, but apparently he was not to be provoked. He simply continued with the self-appointed task, silent and cool, not speaking at all until he had handed her a cup.

'Getting married is now a matter of instant priority,' he informed her as he stood and looked down at her.

'I don't know what you're talking about,' Cassy said quickly, her heart beginning to thump. 'We've been through all this before.'

'Under very different circumstances,' he agreed quietly. 'You're pregnant!'

'For goodness' sake!' Cassy muttered heatedly. 'I fainted. Stop being dramatic.'

'Cut it out, Cassy,' he growled. 'I'm not a boy. I've watched you get more and more on edge since Christmas, and the time could be just about right. Come right out and say it's not true if you can, but lying to me is utterly useless! This is something that can't be lied about at all. Time will make things very obvious.'

She got up and walked into the sitting-room, and he followed, standing in the doorway as she looked out of the window, avoiding his eyes.

'I'm looking for another job,' she said quietly. 'I've been doing that since Christmas. Nobody here is going to know.'

'Don't be so damned insulting!' he rasped. 'And don't be so ridiculous. Given the scenario that you were able to get another job and move, how long do you think you could hold it down? What do you intend to do?' he suddenly added with frightening quiet. 'What are you going to do about this baby?'

'I'm going to keep it!' she said fiercely, spinning round and looking at him. 'In this modern day and age...'

'That's my child!' he grated furiously. 'Don't start talking to me about this modern day and age! If you imagine that I'm going to allow you to go off and set up as an unmarried mother, then you can think again.'

'How do you propose to stop me?'

She suddenly had a feeling of how things would have been if Jordan had loved her, the joy they would be feeling now, and it took some of the edge off her voice.

'I'll take it from you,' he said coldly. 'I'm well-known, reasonably wealthy, with a stable home and the ability to give a good many material things to a child. I'll fight you for it, make no mistake about that, Cassy!'

'Do you imagine you'd win?' she asked tremulously, stunned by his vehemence. 'Half your days are spent away in dangerous places.'

'Not any more, they're not!' he assured her bitingly. 'Those days are over. Even if they weren't, they are now.'

Cassy said nothing. The knowledge of how securely Jordan was trapped hit her very hard. It didn't matter now about telling his father that they were just not suited, about breaking it to him that Jordan was intent upon going back to his old life. The whole picture had changed, *she* was now his burden. It was incredible when she thought back to the time, so very close really, when she had first reluctantly invited him here to this flat. He had tried to help her out, and now he was stuck with her.

'Apart from anything else,' he carried on relentlessly, 'we have relatives who are to some extent involved. Your mother...'

'I don't give a damn about what my mother thinks!' Cassy said hotly. 'She can laugh herself into a fit for all I care.'

'My mother and father are not about to do that,' he said quietly. 'They're getting on in years; they would welcome a grandchild. Maybe you don't care what your mother and father think, and maybe they're quite hardened to this sort of thing. My mother and father are not. They expect a loving couple to be married.'

'We're not a loving couple,' Cassy said bitterly, knowing that she was truly boxed into this and seeing no way out of it.

'Then we'll have to pretend that we are,' Jordan snapped. 'Whatever we pretend, though, you're marrying me, Cassy, and you're marrying me immediately. If you refuse, you can get ready for the sky to fall on you!' He strode to the door, turning to glare at her. 'I'm going, but I'll be back at five. By then, have your answer ready!'

She didn't know what to do. If she hadn't loved him so much it would be different, she would have fought every step of the way. She was no fool. The first priority of any court would be to leave a child with its mother. But the publicity, the battling... Jordan's name would be dragged through the mud, his mother and father would be so hurt that they would never recover.

If she gave in and married him, then he would be tied for life to an existence he hated. If she fought, he would be hurt, everyone would be hurt. She was still sitting there, a half-drunk cup of cold tea beside her, even her coat still on, when he came back later.

Evidently it was his lunchtime, and he came straight in, using the key that he had kept, his sudden arrival taking her by surprise. When he had said five, she had believed it. He had caught her off guard without a single thing to say.

'Well?' he rasped, his eyes taking in the fact that she had sat unmoving since he had left her. 'I'm ready to hear every argument you can come up with.'

She didn't answer and he moved closer, his eyes on her pale face.

'Cassy,' he said a little less harshly, 'are you all right?'

For a second she looked up at him, her dark eyes wide and troubled, and then she looked away defeatedly; there was no give in him at all. He had a responsibility and he was going to shoulder it if it killed him.

'I've thought and thought, but everywhere I turn I come up with answers that are going to hurt somebody,' she said faintly. 'I don't know what to do.'

'I do!' he said forcefully, taking her arms and lifting her to her feet. 'The first person who is not going to be hurt is you.'

His softened attitude stunned her and she stood swaying a little, her bewilderment obviously mistaken for another fainting spell as he quickly grasped her again.

'You said you were all right,' he reminded her accusingly.

'I—I'm absolutely glowing with health,' she managed shakily.

'Then get that astonishing fur hat on,' he said wryly. 'I'm taking you out to lunch.'

'The office!' Cassy protested, and by his muttered annoyance she could tell that the thought of the office had completely slipped his mind. He went to her phone and rang in, though, asking for his deputy.

'I'll be out for the rest of the day, Barry,' he announced. 'Any problems can wait until morning.' He listened for a minute and then said, 'Fine, you can cope with that. Put me through to Guy Meredith.'

Cassy wondered what he was going to say, what excuse he was going to give for her, but Jordan's mind never ran to excuses.

'Cassy's not coming back,' he said as soon as he had apparently got Guy at the other end of the phone. 'You're on your own again.' His face tightened for a moment as he listened, and then he rasped, 'Of course she's all right. Don't be so damned motherly!'

'Do you have to speak to Guy like that?' Cassy asked heatedly as he turned back to her.

'Yes, I do,' he grated. His face lost some of its annoyance for a minute as his eyes flared over her. 'Get your Russian hat, it's cold outside,' he growled more softly, 'and if you want Guy for a godfather it's all right by me. Until then, it's my job to look after you—Guy can get on with the paper!'

He didn't need any of Cassy's planning. It was quite clear that, while she had been sitting worriedly in her flat, he had been doing all the planning necessary and he gave no time for thought.

'Do you think your father will want to give you away?' he asked thoughtfully as they ate lunch. It was no use trying to pretend that this was not going to happen, she realised as she glanced quickly and worriedly at his face. She had to go right along with it.

'I—I thought that we'd be having a quiet civil ceremony,' she said anxiously.

'With my mother in on it?' he scoffed with a low laugh. 'Can you really imagine it? Your mother will be in the States, and I suggest that we leave her there—unless you want her?' She shook her head and he continued firmly, 'Then we'll get married from my home. We'll get it all arranged, drive down there the day before and you can leave for the church from there. I'll stay in a hotel for the night.'

'W-when?' Cassy managed, paler than ever. She had been quite used to being a burden for most of her life, but since she had started to work her life had been her own and now she was forced to give it up, to have to face each day knowing that she was a burden to Jordan.

'As soon as possible,' he said determinedly, signalling for the bill. 'We have a house, what's to hold us up?'

She didn't answer, but she knew where they were going as he turned the car out of town and headed for the surrounding countryside. They would have a house. Until now she hadn't had time to consider that. Her mind had vaguely planned a flat in some unknown, unfriendly town. Jordan already had a home of his own and it was going to be hers.

She was reluctant to get out of the car as he drove up the country lane that led to his house and parked on the gravel drive by the white front door.

'Come on, Cassy,' he said gently, getting out and coming round to her. 'There's really nothing to worry about, I promise.'

There was no shred of her previous abrasive character about her now, she acknowledged as she got out of the car and went towards the house. She had been another person, a new person for weeks, and she could not even remember what she used to be like. She felt very vulnerable, tearful and scared.

'I'm going to make a fire,' he said quietly, helping her off with her coat. 'I want you to just wander around the house. I want you to pry into every last thing and then come back down with complaints and ideas. I'll fix everything you don't like.'

He urged her gently out of the hall and she started with the downstairs area, avoiding the sitting-room deliberately. The memories it held were too poignant. She would have to have a better grip on herself before she went in there.

It was a big house, comfortable and beautifully furnished, the kitchen a dream and upstairs it was the same. She felt forlorn, as if she was here under false pretences, as indeed she was, and her heart hammered frighteningly as she stepped unexpectedly into Jordan's bedroom. The whole room sang of him: the colours, the pictures, the lamps, and she was not surprised to see that he slept in a double bed, he was too big and too tall to sleep on any small bed. It reminded her of his nights on her settee, his goodness to her. What was he being now but good to her? She longed for even the quiet companionship they had shared then, but it was all gone now.

He was in the sitting-room when she went back, and there was nothing for it but to brace herself and go in.

'Oh, you took the tree down!' she said a trifle breathlessly, and then blushed as he looked at her with a quizzical expression that bordered on mockery.

'Of course,' he assured her. 'I do know all the right things to do. My mother brought me up carefully to allow for the fairies at the bottom of the garden. The decorations are lovingly saved, the holly has been burned and I know that the tree must be planted but that it must not grow. Did I miss out anything?'

Cassy smiled faintly as she shook her head and went to sit by the fire, looking into the newly leaping flames and not at Jordan. There was a strained silence and then he asked, 'Tell me what to change.'

'Nothing!' She glanced up and as quickly looked away from those silvery eyes that seemed to have gained a new glow from the firelight. 'The whole place is beautiful. The kitchen is a very tempting place and the bathrooms are heaven.'

She was silent again and he waited for further comment, but as she was so clearly not about to make any he said with a suddenly businesslike air, 'I don't have a housekeeper living in. A woman comes in daily, but if you want a housekeeper...'

'No,' Cassy said quickly. 'I'm not used to one now, and I'd rather not. I enjoy cooking, and when I get back from work I can easily...'

'You're not going back to work, Cassy,' he said firmly, his eyes intently on her as she looked up in surprise. 'When I told Guy that you weren't going back, I meant just that. I made a few enquiries this morning when I got back to work after taking you to your flat. With a special licence we can be married at the end of next week. Until then, I want you to spend each day here. You can spend the time in turning this house into a home.'

'You said I wouldn't have to give up anything,' she reminded him accusingly, but he just sat back and looked at her evenly.

'That was before we knew you were pregnant,' he pointed out. 'There's no need for you to work, and I want you to take it easy. You'll not be tied indoors. I'll get you a car and you can do just what you like.'

'Everything except what I want to do!' Cassy said with a flare of mutiny.

'If all you want to do is go to the *Herald* each day, then yes,' he said tightly. 'I want this place to be something other than a bachelor pad when we get back here after the wedding. I have neither the time nor the ability to alter it.' His voice suddenly softened. 'Don't you want a home for the baby, Cassy?' he asked quietly. 'Don't you want it to have a real home?'

She nodded and looked away, all her anger dying. Yes, she did. She wanted that very fiercely; with her background, perhaps a little too fiercely.

'The room that looks out over the hills,' she said quickly, 'the one at the back of the house, has a dressing-room off. It would make a good nursery for the baby and I could sleep there. If I can change things in that room...?'

'Anything you like,' he said coolly, all the softness dying from his face as he stood. 'I told you that you could rearrange anything. In fact, I'll expect you to do just that. I'll leave it to you. Meanwhile, I'll make some coffee and then drive you to your flat. I'll have you a car by the day after tomorrow, and then you can drive yourself over here during the day. I presume you can drive?'

Cassy just nodded, not surprised that she felt like an outsider. She didn't really know Jordan, after all. Here, in his house, listening to him making plans for her life, the whole thing became frightening, especially as she knew he would be filled with resentment and that he would never speak of it.

At least she would have her own room. Obviously he had not expected her to sleep in his room. Perhaps after the baby was born he would agree to a divorce, and they could come to some amicable arrangement. It was the only way that she could think of to set him free and not to hurt too many people, other than herself.

CHAPTER TEN

JORDAN'S parents were stunned, but they were happy. They both wanted to speak to her on the phone when Jordan rang them, and it was so difficult to be natural with Jordan standing there, his face trying to hide the grimness he felt. She handed over to him when the tears in her throat threatened to choke her, and it was marvellous how he managed to sound light-hearted and happy when his face remained utterly stiff.

His parents were thrilled that the wedding would be from their house, though, and true to Jordan's warning Dorothy Reece began at once to organise everything; greatly relieved, Cassy suspected, that the famous and beautiful Lavinia Preston would not be there.

Her father rather startled her with his enthusiasm. He sounded almost as delighted as Harold Reece had done. He wanted all the details, and it was only later that Cassy recalled that none of them had questioned the speed of this, the inappropriate time of the year. They would know eventually. It didn't take too much intelligence to add up to nine.

It was cold on the day. They had driven down in the early part of the previous day, although they could have gone sooner, but Cassy suspected that Jordan didn't want to be there long enough for questions—neither did he fancy a long time of play-acting, and plenty of that was necessary!

'Didn't you want to wait a while, dear, and get married in white?' Dorothy Reece asked as she helped Cassie to dress for the wedding. 'You look absolutely lovely, mind you, but—well, every girl's dream, you know, and mid-February is such dreary weather.'

Cassy looked at herself in the mirror. She had gone as close as she could to every girl's dream. Her woollen suit was cream, the small collar embroidered in gold. Her long hair was caught up behind her head, a thin band of fresh flowers pinned across her hair, the pink and cream delicately contrasting with the burnished mahogany. She hadn't really dreamed of being married in white. Her love for Jordan was so new that she had never had the time to dream of marriage, and even if she had she had always known what Jordan's future was. She had never been in his future. Apart from this sudden and blinding passion he disliked her, had always disliked her. Tears filled her eyes and Dorothy's arm came round her at once.

'You look very beautiful, Cassy,' she said softly. 'You *are* beautiful. We're so fond of you. If I made you cry...'

'No,' Cassy said with a smile, 'I think it's nerves.' She suddenly wanted a friend, any friend, and she looked into the warm, smiling eyes of Jordan's mother. 'I'm pregnant,' she told her quietly.

She had no idea what reaction she had expected. Reactions from her own mother were usually predictable. Lavinia would have said immediately, 'You fool!'

Dorothy Reece stood stunned for a minute, and then her face lit up with happiness.

'Cassy! My dear! I'm so glad! Harold will be thrilled, though of course if you don't want me to tell him yet...?' She suddenly looked a little worried. 'Cassy, you do want...?'

'Of course!' Cassy said simply, a great burden suddenly lifting from her heart. Of course she wanted

Jordan's baby. Her colour came back. The pallor that had worried Dorothy Reece all morning was suddenly not there, and Jordan's mother smiled into her eyes.

'Let's get you to the church, then!' she said happily.

Two months later there was nothing to lift Cassy's heart except the warm secret that was growing inside. From the first, Jordan had been nothing more than pleasant. He was as aloof as he had been when she'd first known him, and it was quite clear that all he wanted was to keep out of her way for most of the time.

She had the house in order, everything organised and running smoothly. Most of her time was spent in trying to make it more and more of a home. There were apparently no restrictions on money at all, and she bought pictures, ornaments, new and comfortable pieces of furniture, her whole mind given up to bringing warmth to a house that daily became more beautiful but slowly grew more cold.

Jordan worked. Little more could be said than that. He was gone before she got up every morning, although she still kept her habit of rising in time for work; and in the evenings he congratulated her on anything she had altered, declared the meals she cooked to be delicious and then retired to his study to type until late. She never discovered what he typed. Morning would find the study scrupulously tidied, the desk drawers locked.

If he was out at some dinner he would ring and tell her politely, or leave an equally polite note where she could find it. It was like living with a flatmate with immaculate manners, and it made her feel like an intruder.

If she had not had a car she would have probably gone mad, but she went to town regularly and often met people she knew. Jean took to arranging her lunchtime break so that they could have lunch together, and Cassy kept abreast with the paper and the general gossip of the office.

She had just left Jean one day when she bumped into Guy Meredith for the first time since she had left work.

'Cass!' He called to her from across the street, dashing over and hugging her enthusiastically. 'How are you, love?' he asked warmly as he propelled her back into the restaurant she had just left. 'You can talk to me while I eat,' he said determinedly when she protested that another lunch would be out of the question, and she was so pleased to see him that she agreed readily enough.

'You're not too busy, are you?' he asked anxiously, after almost forcing her into a chair, and she found herself smiling ruefully.

'No, I'm not busy.' There was a limit to how far you could go in turning a house into a palace. 'Congratulations, by the way, on getting *my* job!'

'You can have it back any time,' he muttered. 'Jordan is . . .' He suddenly stopped, going quite pink, and Cassy smiled wryly.

'Don't mind me, Guy. Hold nothing back. I'm still one of the boys!'

'He's working himself to death,' Guy told her sombrely. 'Mind you, that's his affair and he's big and strong enough to take it, although I think he's looking a bit thin round the edges lately. Trouble is, he's the only Superman there, and he's working all of us to death too. We'll probably crack up first.' He shot a look at her and then went back to his lunch. 'I wish you hadn't left, Cass. I honestly think he hates the office now that you're not there.'

It wasn't that, although she could hardly tell Guy. Jordan hated everything now because he was trapped for life. She hardly heard anything else that Guy said. An old thought reasserted itself and she faced it squarely. Jordan must have some hope. She couldn't leave it any longer.

Guy walked with her to her car after lunch, a little of his gloom lifted, and he stood looking at her affectionately as she prepared to leave.

'Shall I tell you something, Cass?' he asked, and she laughed across at him.

'I expect you will!' she assured him.

'It's serious,' he said. 'Before Jordan came, I spent most of my time thinking about you, Cass. I had this dream that one day you'd marry me. I suppose I'd have asked you if I hadn't been a bit scared of the sharp edge of your tongue. I never expected though that you and Jordan...'

'Oh, Guy!' Cassy walked back round to where he stood at the other side of her car and automatically he took her hand. 'I had no idea! If I've made you unhappy...'

'No, Cass,' he said softly. 'Just don't stop being a friend, that's all.'

'I never will,' Cassy said gently, and he leaned forward to kiss her cheek just as she looked up and saw Jordan's Porsche cruising past. Their eyes met and Jordan's eyes were as Luigi had once said, like icy seas.

He was parked in front of the house when she got back, and she hurried inside to find him making coffee for himself.

'I didn't know you were coming back for lunch,' she said quickly, wishing she had known so that she could have made something special.

'I'm not,' he answered coolly. 'I've come to change. There's a meeting this afternoon at the *Gazette* offices and then another meeting later. I won't be in to dinner.'

'We'll have it later...' Cassy began, but he cut her off abruptly.

'I'll eat out!'

He turned and strode out of the kitchen, leaving his coffee, and she was still staring at him forlornly when he suddenly stopped and looked back.

'If you're meeting Meredith, do you mind not doing it so openly?' he rasped.

Cassy's cheeks flushed as she stared at him. 'I'm not meeting Guy!'

'I have perfect eyesight!' he grated, the eyes in question icily on her. 'Kissing an old acquaintance in the street is not what I expect of you.'

'I saw Guy today by chance,' she said heatedly, her temper rising at this unfair accusation. 'It's the first time I've seen him since...since...'

'Since you fainted in the office and he went for me!' he finished for her. 'I hope you explained to him that you're already married and that it's a little too late for him?' he added coldly.

'I didn't have to explain anything to Guy,' Cassy said bitterly. 'He already knows that I'm married, and anyone with reasonable eyesight can see that I'm pregnant!'

His eyes swept over her coldly, his lips twisting into the mockery of a smile.

'It's early days yet. You don't look nearly as pregnant as you will look!' he assured her harshly, and tears flooded into her eyes almost at once as she turned away. Clearly he enjoyed torturing himself, and her.

'Cassy!' He took a step towards her but she swung back, her face controlled.

'Don't let me keep you,' she said with a coldness to match his own. 'Guy says that you're working yourself to death,' she added deliberately. 'I'd hate to stop you!'

Jordan left, his face pale and grim, and she kept out of his way until she heard the Porsche pull away from the house. It was the first time that they had actually quarrelled outright since their marriage, and in some obscure way it was a relief. She would rather have him wildly angry than cool and polite. When he came back, she would tell him her decision.

It was eleven when he came home, but Cassy was still up. She put on her dressing-gown to go downstairs to face him. She had bought herself a new dressing-gown. Soon the other would be too tight. Nothing showed much as yet, except to herself, but she tried to keep her condition inconspicuous in front of Jordan. There was no need to be a constant reminder to him that he was trapped into this. Her robe was full and flowing, and after one anxious sideways glance at herself she went down to face him.

Whether he had eaten or not she could not tell, but he was pouring himself a drink in the sitting-room and he looked up in surprise as she came in.

'I want to talk to you, Jordan,' she said determinedly before her nerve gave out.

'Can't it wait?' he asked irritably after one look at her face. 'Working yourself to death is tiring, as you can imagine,' he added sarcastically.

Cassy's face flushed but she was determined to get this out now.

'It won't take long,' she assured him coldly, and he inclined his head towards a chair, advising her apparently to sit. Her nerve didn't quite run to that, so she stood facing him.

'When the baby is born,' she said quietly, 'I want a divorce!'

For a moment he just stood quite still and looked at her, no expression on his face, but a peculiar look in his eyes that frightened her.

'Had it not been for the baby,' she hurried on, 'we would never have been married, and nothing really is changed. Clearly we still feel about each other as we did before, and I can't see why we should be locked in misery for life.'

'I had already asked you to marry me,' he reminded her with too much quiet in his voice. 'You also know that I'll fight for the baby. I told you that.'

'You'll not win,' Cassy said with as much calm as she could muster, 'and there's no need for that. You could see it as often as you wanted. Maybe if we weren't married we—we would be friends and...'

'You've got a friend!' Jordan bit out. 'Or does Meredith plan to be more than that when this mythological divorce takes place? Tell him, hard luck! He missed the boat.'

'This has nothing to do with Guy!' Cassy snapped exasperatedly. She was trying to help, to let Jordan go, and all he could do was keep on about Guy. It was the typical attitude of a man: not even willing to give up something he didn't want himself.

'Well, it's everything to do with me and the answer is no,' Jordan stated. 'If you're tired of pretending to be a wife, then get a housekeeper! If you think I'm letting you go so that afterwards this child can be left while you get back to the life of a busy newshound, then you're mistaken. I expect you've picked out the Swiss finishing school already!'

The cruelty overwhelmed her and she simply turned away to walk to the door, tears swimming in her eyes.

'Cassy!' He was there long before her and he spun her into his arms. 'I'm sorry. That was a rotten thing to say!'

It was the first time he had touched her since the wedding, and every part of Cassy's body reacted with hunger as he pulled her close. Tears streamed down her face and he stroked her cheeks, wiping them away before pulling her head to his shoulder.

'I'm sorry, Cassy,' he said softly, his whole body tight, and she knew why. Close to her, of course, her pregnancy was very obvious. She managed wonderfully well to keep it hidden, but he couldn't touch her and be unaware of it. She pulled away hastily, turning and walking out.

'I can cope with harsh words,' she said tautly. 'Just don't touch me, please.'

He neither followed nor spoke, and she raced to her room and locked the door, wondering how she could keep this up in the months that would follow.

Next morning he was still there as she came into the kitchen. Her 'daily' had this day off, and she had come down quickly to get started on a few things that needed doing. Her face flushed with surprise and embarrassment when she saw Jordan sitting at the kitchen table with a cup of tea.

He looked straight at her and she didn't know what to say. She was wearing a skirt she had already abandoned as the waistband was too tight; it wasn't even fastened properly. Her blouse too was at its last stage of usefulness, her blossoming breasts surging against it. It was the first time ever that he had caught her off guard, and her hand went automatically to fasten her skirt, her face flushed as his eyes followed her nervous movement.

'Too tight?' he asked amusedly, and she flushed even more as she fled from the room and ran quickly upstairs to hide until he'd gone.

She would never be caught like that again, she vowed angrily, throwing her blouse on to the bed. Sooner or later it would be very noticeable, but by then she would have got used to Jordan's cold ways and maybe it wouldn't matter so much. She slipped the skirt off and tossed it beside the blouse, and at that moment Jordan simply walked in without knocking.

'What did I say?' he began angrily, his face changing as he saw her standing there in her bra and panties, her whole attitude one of flight and horror. She snatched up her skirt, her face white with shock, and he came slowly into the room, his silver eyes holding hers.

'You're embarrassed with me?' he asked, softly unbelieving. 'You're shy? Is that what it's all about? Is that why you ran off last night?'

'No! No—I . . .' The colour flooded back into her face and she stood there at bay as he came slowly towards her. 'Jordan, please go out! Please. I . . .'

'Don't you know how beautiful you are?' he asked gently, standing in front of her with no intention of leaving. 'Don't you realise how much more beautiful this has made you? Your skin is glowing, your hair shines twice as much, you've got a wonderful soft look in your eyes. For the first time since I've met you, you look utterly vulnerable and gentle.' He took the skirt from her lifeless fingers and tossed it back to the bed, his eyes roaming hungrily over her. 'Daily, in front of my astonished eyes, you're blossoming,' he murmured, his fingers trailing down her arms. 'Quietly and secretly you're turning into everything that makes a woman mystical.'

His eyes slowly traced her whole body, his gaze sensuous and intent. Cassy stood unmoving, her heart beating frantically as his fingers gently unclipped her bra and let it fall to the floor.

'Don't you know how exciting you are to me like this?' he breathed, his voice thick. His hands lifted to shape her breasts carefully, staying there as he lifted his head and looked at her with drugged eyes. 'I've never wanted you so much,' he whispered.

Cassy was trembling all over, his drowsy voice reaching to the very core of her, his warm hands filling her with growing hunger, and her own hands came to cover his as she looked up at him with wide, wondering eyes.

'Jordan, I don't want to...' She was about to say that she didn't want to trap him, but he mistook her words, although even that didn't make him angry, didn't bring him back into the world.

'I want to,' he said huskily, 'and if I don't, I'll go quietly mad!'

He pulled her gently to the bed, lowering her to the cool sheets, standing over her as he pulled his shirt impatiently over his head, regardless of buttons. It was the first time ever she had seen him undress, and his eyes roamed over her all the time. He was so powerful that her heart missed a beat, but he was beside her before she could even begin to feel fear, and those eyes that could be so frostily cold were dark with passion as he ran his hands over her slowly, moving the last garment that hid her from his feverish gaze.

'Cassy!' he said thickly, his breath harsh in his throat. 'Tell me you want this. Don't leave me guessing. This time, don't leave me with the feeling that I've tricked you into it. I need to know, Cassy!'

'Jordan!' She turned hungrily into his arms, feeling him tremble against her, astonished at his need, her hands running over his skin that was already burning, and his lips claimed hers fiercely as he moulded her tightly to him.

'Help me to be gentle,' he groaned. 'I'm desperate for you, Cassy!'

She didn't want him to be gentle. Within seconds she was on fire, her ardour forcing a gasp of pleasure and protest from him as his lips closed over her breast, and they both forgot her condition as the whole world went up in flames.

He murmured her name against her lips, trying to slow her down, but she was spinning again on the very edge of the world, calling to him in the same far-away voice, her eyes staring into the burning silver of his, and he grasped her tightly, giving her the fierce possession she begged for, holding her as she swirled into darkness and back into light.

He was watching her as she drifted back to the present, his eyes on her flushed, wild face. He cupped her head with one hand and kept on looking at her and she couldn't look away. His free hand caressed her breasts and the silken swell of her stomach, his legs locked with hers.

'This time,' he said slowly, his voice still shaken with passion, 'I'll not let you move. I won't even let you speak. This time, you'll not take heaven away from me. I've been there again, just as I went before, but this time I'm keeping it.'

Cassy gazed up at him, stunned by the vibrancy of his voice, shaken by the look in his eyes.

'Jordan,' she began, but his hand tightened on her head, his eyes almost threatening.

'Not unless it's good,' he warned softly. 'Not unless you're telling me something I want to hear.'

They both heard something they didn't want to hear at that moment. A car came to a stop outside the house, the door slamming, and a finger was placed firmly on the bell.

'Who the hell...?' Jordan began as he moved, and Cassy leapt up, ignoring the stars that suddenly swam in front of her as she grabbed her robe and slipped into it to cross to the window and look down at the car.

'It—it's my mother!' she gasped.

'I don't believe it!' Jordan exclaimed, and then he began to search angrily for his clothes. 'I'm just in the mood for Lavinia,' he grated, and Cassy fled, hastily fastening her robe and racing down to get to the door, to get her word in first.

'Watch those stairs!' Jordan rapped out furiously, and the angry sound gave her a small burst of hope.

She opened the door and Lavinia swept in, making unerringly for the sitting-room and a good background for her act.

'How did you...?' Cassy began in a bewildered voice, but she got no further. Lavinia had come to speak and that was that.

'Your father,' she enlightened. 'Apparently he was at the wedding?'

'You were in New York,' Cassy said, suddenly guilty.

'Oh, don't worry, darling!' Lavinia said, smiling. 'I couldn't possibly have come. I've got exactly one day and then I'm back there. I needed to see you so I flew over.'

'To see me?' Cassy asked a little stupidly.

'Of course! Isn't that what I just said?' Lavinia asked with a slight exasperation, turning to face her.

Her eyes suddenly focused sharply.

'You're pregnant!' she said furiously as Cassy flushed.

'And married!' Jordan said with equal fury, walking in at that moment and coming to stand with his arm around Cassy's shoulders.

'So I understand,' Lavinia said calmly, her eyes on Jordan with no sign of her seductive act. 'News does reach me, you know.'

'Providing it can travel fast enough!' Jordan bit out, and Lavinia showed signs of temper for once.

'I want to speak to Cassandra alone,' she said tightly. 'Can you allow us a minute?'

'No!' Jordan rasped immediately, but Cassy looked up at him pleadingly and he looked into her eyes for a second before releasing her. 'All right,' he said quietly, 'but only until I've made some coffee.'

'Possessive,' Lavinia said in amusement as he walked out. She sat down with an abrupt movement that was not at all like her, and looked up at Cassy. 'Do you love him?'

'Yes.' There was no need to be more emphatic. A simple reply was quite enough. She did love him, tenderly, deeply, wildly, every way it was possible to love.

'Thank heaven for that!' Lavinia sat back and gave Cassy a green-eyed look of amusement. 'Well, he's certainly not letting go of you. He's the first man I couldn't handle. He doesn't react to me at all until I annoy him,' she finished with a look of astonishment.

It infuriated Cassy. This was why she had been forced to leave Jordan's arms? To come down here to a mother who never made her presence felt unless she was after something?

'I should think you have quite enough admirers, without wanting my husband to join the simpering ranks,' she said heatedly.

The perfect eyebrows raised in surprise.

'What are you suggesting?' she asked coolly.

'You took Luigi!' Cassy said violently as Jordan walked back into the room, stopping at the door as he heard Cassy's voice. 'You also fluttered your lashes at Jordan. I would have thought one lover at a time was enough!'

Lavinia stood slowly, her normal well-planned grace leaving her in anger.

'As you're pregnant,' she said angrily, 'I won't walk across and slap you for that remark. Instead, I'll explain to you how stupid you are. You imagined yourself in love with Luigi. You knew nothing about him but what he had told you. Well, I knew something about him, but one look at your face that holiday assured me that it was useless to tell you. People imagine that we see nothing beyond the footlights; they're wrong! I used to see Luigi Rosato, night after night. I used to see him at the restaurants I visited, waiting to catch my eye, accidentally arriving as I did. I never looked at him but he began to annoy me, and I did wonder how he managed to keep on paying the bills. I don't dine cheaply.' She sat down again and so did Cassy, her legs suddenly weak.

Jordan came forward and sat on the arm of Cassy's chair, his hand against her shoulder, and Lavinia looked at them both for a second before she went on.

'I became intrigued, so I had a few discreet enquiries made. Luigi Rosato, small, insignificant parts in Italian theatre, little talent, big ego. Source of income—selling drugs!'

Cassy's face went white and Jordan tightened his hand on her shoulder, but her mother went on relentlessly.

'Having obviously decided that I was not about to notice him and take him under my wing, he disappeared, to my great joy. Imagine my surprise and annoyance, my horror, when he resurfaced with my own daughter!' She sprang up and began to pace about, nothing dramatic about her, only fury in the beautiful voice. 'How I watched you that holiday, my girl! I dreaded that he had persuaded you into the filthy habit. He takes nothing himself, but he was doing quite well because he managed to keep up with my life-style and clearly could afford to take a course at college. You were all right, though. So I decided to teach him a lesson and get you out of the picture. He only took up with you to get to me, he's a remarkably single-minded little snake. He wants his name in lights, preferably *over* my own!' she added in astonishment.

She looked across at them.

'I had to get you down there to see him. I wanted to see how you reacted to him, to see if there was any way at all he could get to you again.' She burst into laughter. 'You came with Jordan Reece, with a great big ring on your finger and a possessive arm around your waist. Jordan reacted to me not at all, he doted on you, and I could have screamed for joy! I came here today just to make quite sure, and I'm quite sure. You can serve me some coffee now,' she said with an imperious look at Jordan, and to Cassy's astonishment he got up and did just that.

'Does—did you tell Daddy?' Cassy asked as they sat almost silently watching her mother.

'Giles? Good heavens, no!' Lavinia exclaimed. 'He would have waded in furiously and made matters worse.

Your father has no finesse whatever. No, I had to do it myself and I took a very malicious delight in doing it. Now I can drop him on his smooth, dark head.' She threw her own beautiful head back and sighed. 'I never again wish to hear that word "*cara*". That wretch has spoiled a most lovely word!'

'Why didn't you just tell me?' Cassy asked in little more than a whisper.

'How could I, darling?' Lavinia said impatiently, rising and pulling on her gloves. 'We were never close.' She paused at the door and looked at Cassy for a second before leaning to peck at her cheek. 'A grandchild!' she murmured in disgust. 'I'll have to start taking older parts.'

She was gone before they realised it. She had always had so much presence that everyone was left subdued after her departure, but this time she had turned over the past like a newly ploughed field, and Cassy still stood staring at the door.

Jordan stood at the window, his back tight with anger, his whole attitude suggesting that he would never speak again.

'She—she actually cares,' Cassy said in a bewildered voice, wondering why he was so very angry.

'After her fashion,' he grated, turning away, his shoulders tense, every line of his body telling her of his rage. 'I could kill anyone who hurts you,' he ground out. 'I've always felt like that, which is laughable considering that I hurt you more than anyone!'

'You haven't hurt me,' Cassy assured him quietly. She was still bewildered by events, by his lovemaking and the things he had said, by her mother's revelations. 'When I have the baby...'

'Stop calling it "the baby"!' he rasped, turning on her with furious eyes. 'It's *my* baby!'

Cassy looked at him for a second, stunned at the raw emotion racing across his normally impassive face. Maybe this wasn't the time to speak to him, after all. He was too enraged, too tight inside.

'It—it doesn't matter,' she said a little anxiously. 'I'll talk to you later.'

'Talk to me now!' he snapped.

She looked at him rather tragically, loving him so much but unable to approach him now. Everything had gone so terribly wrong in the past. She wanted him to be happy, no matter what it meant to her. He saw the look on her face and his expression was if possible more bleak.

'Lord, how trapped a woman must feel at a time like this,' he said bitterly. 'Here I am, enraged that your mother can only care about you in that cold, quite practical manner, but I'm the one who trapped you. I'm the one who made you pregnant!'

'I—I want to have your baby,' she said simply. 'I always have.'

'Cassy?' He looked at her as if she was suddenly mad, and she rushed on before he could stop her.

'When it's born,' she said rapidly, 'I don't want a divorce. I want to stay here. I'll not hold you back, Jordan. I'll just—just be here so that when you get back from—from any place, you'll have a home ready and you'll be able to see your baby and enjoy it and...'

'Where do you think I'm going?' He stood looking at her intently, his eyes more strange than ever, glitteringly silver, hypnotising her.

'You—you'll be going overseas. When this is all settled there'll be no reason to stay behind, and...'

'You think I want to leave you?' he said tautly. 'You think I could? Are you anxious to have the house to yourself, Cassy?'

'I—I don't want to keep you here,' she said tremulously. 'I don't want to be the one who holds you back from the things you want.'

'You've kept me here from the moment I first saw you,' he told her quietly. 'I made no promises when I came to look around with Dad. I saw you and suddenly nothing else seemed exciting any more. I stayed for you, Cassy, not for anything or anyone else. You don't hold me back from the things I want. I couldn't get anywhere near you, and it was more than clear that you hated me, but right from the first the only thing I wanted was you.'

'Jordan?' She stood dazed, unable to believe what he was saying, the room beginning to spin.

'Don't you dare faint!' he said shakily, his arms coming round her as he leapt forward. 'I haven't finished yet.' He held her gently, looking into her eyes. 'For better or for worse, you're stuck with me, Cassy. I love you, darling!' He smiled at her ruefully. 'Now you can faint,' he added mockingly.

'Oh, Jordan, Jordan, I love you so much!' Tears flooded down her face and she flung her arms around his neck.

'Are you sure?' he asked in a bemused voice, and she was suddenly laughing through the tears, happiness soaring.

'Of course I'm sure! Do you dare to imagine I would have let you make love to me if I hadn't loved you?' she demanded with a happy imitation of her old manner.

'Cass is back to normal,' he said, smiling into her eyes and then gathering her close to him. 'Oh, Cassy,' he whispered against her hair, 'I love you like a mad fool, I could never be away from you!'

Minutes later, when Cassy was breathless with kisses, Jordan at last drew back.

'You haven't eaten yet!' he said in a shocked voice. 'You must be hungry. I have to feed you two.'

'I'll get it,' Cassy laughed, but he would hear none of that and sat her at the kitchen table where he could see her all the time as he insisted upon getting her breakfast.

'You're late for work,' Cassy suddenly said, glancing at the clock, but he was not at all put out.

'Today work can take care of itself. I'm taking care of you,' he said firmly. 'Besides,' he added, 'your mother interrupted something. We have to go back upstairs and finish it. Then we're going to move all your things from that lonely room and put them into my lonely room. From now on you're with me, Cassy Reece!'

Cassy smiled happily. She knew she would be smiling for the rest of her life, and as she ate her breakfast Jordan sat opposite, simply looking at her, his chin on his hand, all the love she had ever dreamed of in his eyes.

'If we hadn't needed to get engaged for your father...' she began.

'We didn't!' Jordan said promptly. 'He wanted to see you and I promised to try and get you to go, but when you told me about Luigi I was scared that you'd find out you still loved him. I hadn't got you, but I was terrified of losing you completely. Fast action seemed to be called for. It gave me the chance to be with you, to get close to you. It was a good excuse for holding you and kissing you, too,' he finished with a grin.

'You were very good to me,' Cassy said with a sigh, 'especially when I was ill.'

'I wanted to move you in here with me right then,' Jordan told her softly. 'I wanted to take care of you and not let anyone else come close to you.'

'I wasn't meeting Guy,' Cassy said anxiously, and his hand covered hers warmly.

'I know,' he assured her with a grimace. 'That was my frustration coming out. Anyhow, didn't I tell you he could be a godfather?'

'I've hardly seen you since we've been married,' Cassy accused softly, and he leaned forward to kiss her hand.

'I know. I wanted you too much to stay close. I was beginning to think that I'd imagined the way you reacted to me. You wanted a room of your own and I'd caused you enough misery. I've been busy, too,' he added, glancing at her keenly. 'I've been asked to do another book, and also we're taking on two new papers, extending the chain. It's taken a lot of meetings and a lot of travelling, but it's all set up now. In a couple of months I'll be giving up my job at the *Herald* and simply be managing the whole group. It means I'll be able to get on with my book and I'll be here more with you.'

'Oh, Jordan, that's wonderful!' Cassy exclaimed happily.

He stood up and came round to help her to her feet. 'You've finished your breakfast, Mrs Reece,' he said determinedly. 'No more slacking. I'm not wasting this wonderful day!'

'I'm not even dressed yet,' Cassy protested, but his low laugh sent shivers down her spine.

'That can wait,' he said softly.

Jordan drove through the snow that covered the drive as another Christmas came.

'Bet you Dad's been nursing Timothy all the time we've been shopping,' he said with a smile at Cassy.

'I'm not taking that one up,' she laughed. 'Since they came up for Christmas your father's been hanging round the carry-cot in a really stealthy manner. It's a miracle that Timothy sleeps at all.'

He helped her out and they trudged to the door, their arms filled with gaily wrapped parcels.

'I've developed a great liking for snow,' Jordan said softly, stopping to kiss her. 'If it hadn't been for the snow, things would have taken a lot longer—and I wasn't sure how much longer I could wait. I might just have been forced to grab you!'

They entered the house in a flurry of snow and happy laughter, just in time to see Harold Reece hurrying to put the baby down.

'Guess what?' Dorothy said eagerly. 'You had visitors but they couldn't stay. Your mother and father came! Your mother wanted to see the baby.'

'I hope she didn't hold him,' Jordan muttered, helping Cassy off with her coat. 'I'm not at all sure she's capable.'

'Well, your father let her have him for a minute, but he hovered around anxiously all the time!' Jordan's mother told him with a wry look at her husband. 'Anyhow,' she informed Cassy excitedly as Cassy stood stunned at this news, 'they couldn't stay because they're off back to America. Your mother's play is being turned into a film and she's got the leading role. Your father's in it,' she finished triumphantly.

'Not the leading man?' Cassy gasped, unable to see her mother allowing that.

'He's a Southern colonel,' Harold Reece said firmly, his face lighting up with a truly impish grin.

'A Southern colonel,' Cassy mused, her head on one side. 'Yes, I can see that, he could do it!'

'So your grandma is going to be a film star now!' Jordan informed his sleeping son as he walked over to look down at him.

'Oh, don't call her that, Jordan!' Cassy laughed. 'She's going to hate it if Timothy calls her anything other than Lavinia.'

'I suppose so,' Jordan murmured, coming back and putting his arms around her. 'In any case, I don't feel so annoyed with her now. It's partly thanks to her weird ways that I've got you; only partly, though,' he added softly.

'I fail to see how... if we hadn't had to go...' Cassy began, lowering her voice to exclude anyone else.

'I told you,' he murmured against her ear. 'I had every intention of grabbing you if all else failed!'

'You wouldn't have got very far with that,' Cassy said spiritedly, leaning back to look at him defiantly.

'I think I would,' he informed her softly. 'Later I'll prove it!'

PASSPORT TO ROMANCE VACATION SWEEPSTAKES

OFFICIAL RULES

SWEEPSTAKES RULES AND REGULATIONS. NO PURCHASE NECESSARY.

HOW TO ENTER:

1. To enter, complete this official entry form and return with your invoice in the envelope provided, or print your name, address, telephone number and age on a plain piece of paper and mail to: Passport to Romance, P.O. Box #1397, Buffalo, N.Y. 14269-1397. No mechanically reproduced entries accepted.
2. All entries must be received by the Contest Closing Date, midnight, December 31, 1990 to be eligible.
3. Prizes: There will be ten (10) Grand Prizes awarded, each consisting of a choice of a trip for two people to: i) London, England (approximate retail value $5,050 U.S.); ii) England, Wales and Scotland (approximate retail value $6,400 U.S.); iii) Caribbean Cruise (approximate retail value $7,300 U.S.); iv) Hawaii (approximate retail value $ 9,550 U.S.); v) Greek Island Cruise in the Mediterranean (approximate retail value $12,250 U.S.); vi) France (approximate retail value $7,300 U.S.).
4. Any winner may choose to receive any trip or a cash alternative prize of $5,000.00 U.S. in lieu of the trip.
5. Odds of winning depend on number of entries received.
6. A random draw will be made by Nielsen Promotion Services, an independent judging organization on January 29, 1991, in Buffalo, N.Y., at 11:30 a.m. from all eligible entries received on or before the Contest Closing Date. Any Canadian entrants who are selected must correctly answer a time-limited, mathematical skill-testing question in order to win. Quebec residents may submit any litigation respecting the conduct and awarding of a prize in this contest to the Régie des loteries et courses du Quebec.
7. Full contest rules may be obtained by sending a stamped, self-addressed envelope to: "Passport to Romance Rules Request", P.O. Box 9998, Saint John, New Brunswick, E2L 4N4.
8. Payment of taxes other than air and hotel taxes is the sole responsibility of the winner.
9. Void where prohibited by law.

- -

PASSPORT TO ROMANCE VACATION SWEEPSTAKES

OFFICIAL RULES

SWEEPSTAKES RULES AND REGULATIONS. NO PURCHASE NECESSARY.

HOW TO ENTER:

1. To enter, complete this official entry form and return with your invoice in the envelope provided, or print your name, address, telephone number and age on a plain piece of paper and mail to: Passport to Romance, P.O. Box #1397, Buffalo, N.Y. 14269-1397. No mechanically reproduced entries accepted.
2. All entries must be received by the Contest Closing Date, midnight, December 31, 1990 to be eligible.
3. Prizes: There will be ten (10) Grand Prizes awarded, each consisting of a choice of a trip for two people to: i) London, England (approximate retail value $5,050 U.S.); ii) England, Wales and Scotland (approximate retail value $6,400 U.S.); iii) Caribbean Cruise (approximate retail value $7,300 U.S.); iv) Hawaii (approximate retail value $ 9,550 U.S.); v) Greek Island Cruise in the Mediterranean (approximate retail value $12,250 U.S.); vi) France (approximate retail value $7,300 U.S.).
4. Any winner may choose to receive any trip or a cash alternative prize of $5,000.00 U.S. in lieu of the trip.
5. Odds of winning depend on number of entries received.
6. A random draw will be made by Nielsen Promotion Services, an independent judging organization on January 29, 1991, in Buffalo, N.Y., at 11:30 a.m. from all eligible entries received on or before the Contest Closing Date. Any Canadian entrants who are selected must correctly answer a time-limited, mathematical skill-testing question in order to win. Quebec residents may submit any litigation respecting the conduct and awarding of a prize in this contest to the Régie des loteries et courses du Quebec.
7. Full contest rules may be obtained by sending a stamped, self-addressed envelope to: "Passport to Romance Rules Request", P.O. Box 9998, Saint John, New Brunswick, E2L 4N4.
8. Payment of taxes other than air and hotel taxes is the sole responsibility of the winner.
9. Void where prohibited by law.

 RLS-DIR

VACATION SWEEPSTAKES

MONTH 2 ENTRY

Official Entry Form

Yes, enter me in the drawing for one of ten Vacations-for-Two! If I'm a winner, I'll get my choice of any of the six different destinations being offered — and I won't have to decide until after I'm notified!

Return entries with invoice in envelope provided along with Daily Travel Allowance Voucher. Each book in your shipment has two entry forms — and the more you enter, the better your chance of winning!

Name ______________________________

Address ______________________________ Apt.

City ______________ State/Prov. ______________ Zip/Postal Code

Daytime phone number ______________________________
Area Code

☐ I am enclosing a Daily Travel Allowance Voucher in the amount of $__________ Write in amount revealed beneath scratch-off

---

PASSPORT
WIN
1 of 10 Vacations
SEE INSIDE
TO ROMANCE

VACATION SWEEPSTAKES

MONTH 2 ENTRY

Official Entry Form

Yes, enter me in the drawing for one of ten Vacations-for-Two! If I'm a winner, I'll get my choice of any of the six different destinations being offered — and I won't have to decide until after I'm notified!

Return entries with invoice in envelope provided along with Daily Travel Allowance Voucher. Each book in your shipment has two entry forms — and the more you enter, the better your chance of winning!

Name ______________________________

Address ______________________________ Apt.

City ______________ State/Prov. ______________ Zip/Postal Code

Daytime phone number ______________________________
Area Code

☐ I am enclosing a Daily Travel Allowance Voucher in the amount of $__________ Write in amount revealed beneath scratch-off

CPS-TWO